EBENEZER SCROOGE AND THE BATTLE FOR CHRISTMAS

By Michael Mallory

Cushing & Neville
Los Angeles

D1534260

This is a work of fiction. Names, characters, events and incidents are the products of the author's imagination. Any resemblance to actual persons, living or dead, or actual events is purely coincidental.

For Carol Sperling

PROLOGUE

The tall, elegantly-dressed man strode out of the warmth of the public house in the small village and into the freezing cold of the December night. He tightened his scarf and pressed his bell-crowned hat further down on his head to prevent any internal warmth from escaping his body. Despite his physical discomfort, Jasper Crimp walked with a sense of intense satisfaction. He was eminently pleased with himself for a job well done.

Crimp had entered the pub——one of nearly two-dozen he had visited in as many days and in as many different villages——to find the workingmen inside in joyous celebration, reveling in good drink, dining on savory sausages and meat pies, and enjoying each other's presence and conversation. It took very little time for that chatter to lead to the anticipation of Christmas, which was two days hence. Patiently listening to the anticipation of the various crofters, smiths, and tradesmen, whose occupations were revealed through their mode of dress, Crimp had waited for the proper moment to become the focus of attention and offer to buy a round of drink to every man in the pub.

When the cheer that had gone up abated, Jasper Crimp went to work. His silky, persuasive voice was commanding even when heard barely above a whisper. He challenged the proposition that Christmas was anything than yet another day of the year, with no intrinsic powers of joy, happiness, or redemption. Deftly and skillfully, he went from man to man, parrying every argument with a counter thrust,

1

hammering home the notion that only children and fools would celebrate December the 25th, knowing that December the 26th, and every day beyond for the next year, would signify the return of toil, care, and weariness. As cunningly as a barrister, Crimp argued that the reality of life's harshness was not eradicated by Christmas, merely masked, waiting to pounce again once the roasted chestnuts were consumed and the packages torn open.

"Surely you are not children, my friends," he told them, as he always told the men in the pubs he visited. "Surely you are not feeble of mind. You must see the absurdity of singling out one day in a year and ascribing to it an importance that it does not deserve, only to have that false feeling of happiness yanked away as soon as the midnight bell finishes tolling on the morning of the 26th."

Were he in charge, Jasper Crimp had concluded, Christmas would be consigned to the dustbin of history, abolished and ultimately forgotten. By the time he had finished, all of the villagers' high spirits and feelings of merriment had been extinguished like candles. Their heads bowed by the weight of Crimp's words, each man had looked into the empty glass in his hand, unable to respond.

As he had done so many times before, Jasper Crimp had driven a stake through the heart of Christmas for the men of the village. Then, once his task was finished, he bade every man good evening, and took his leave.

As he walked down the cold, dark road away from the heart of the village, Crimp's breath resembled the effluent from a steam engine. But the night suddenly got even darker and colder as an impenetrable shadow fell over him, keeping up with his every step.

You have done well this night, said the voice of the frozen wind.

"Thank you, my lord," Crimp replied, bowing his head in practiced obsequiousness.

There is still more for you to do.

2

"I understand. I will not fail you."

The shadow lifted, revealing once more the stars overhead and the waning moon, which provided just enough light for Crimp to find his way back to his place of lodging. He was once more able to think freely, knowing that even private thought was dangerous when under the cloak of the dark shadow. While appreciative of the approval, he did not need his Master to tell him he had done well. This had been one of his bigger successes. Those fools in the pub would never see the 25th of December the same way again.

There was no one else around on that dark night, not a person, not a shadow, even an owl in the tree or a horse in the field, to see Jasper Crimp's shark smile as he wrapped self-congratulations around himself to further ward off the cold.

ONE

In truth, it did not seem like Christmas.

A persistent, sooty fog hung like a shroud over the streets and buildings of London, enveloping the city like a damp, grey overcoat. Instead of a cleansing December snow, there was only a thick, chilling mist. The moods of the Londoners as they went about their somber business matched the climate. Whereas two men might previously have greeted each other on the street with tips of their hats and heartfelt wishes of goodwill for the holidays, they now exchanged furtive glances and nods. Whereas the chorus of mongers and sellers, each with their distinctive call, would once have filled the streets, lanes, and courts, now there was only the nasal grumbling of work horses. In place of good cheer, the people of London felt gloom; in place of gaiety, they experienced melancholy; in place of bustle, naught but stillness. The city known for its great cacophony of life had fallen silent, and a terrible silence it was.

As though seeking to counteract the silence and gloom, the last happy man in London cheerfully strode through the streets of the city in which he had been born, and which he loved, even though he had been away from her for nearly five years. Fred Billings whistled as his booted feet splashed through puddles, and he doffed his hat to everyone he passed. Part of the reason for his mood of good will was that, even in its depressed condition, London was a welcome sight. An even larger reason was simply that

4

Nature had blessed Fred Billings with an indomitably cheerful spirit.

The grin on his face broadened into a full smile as he rounded a corner and his destination came into view. It was a smallish building tucked inside the narrow passageway of St. Michael's Alley. Changes had been made to the old place since Fred had last seen it: a fresh coat of paint now adorned the ancient wood of the façade and the panes of the front window were now kept scrupulously clean, allowing the light from inside to glow outward. A new sign over the door proclaimed the business partnership of *Scrooge and Cratchit*, replacing the one that for years had announced *Scrooge and Marley*, even long after Marley's death.

As the bell of St. Michael's Cornhill pealed, Fred Billings pulled his watch from his waistcoat pocket, happy to learn that his timepiece was in perfect agreement with the church's: it was four o'clock. Returning the repeater to its nest, Fred pushed open the door of Scrooge and Cratchit's counting house (silently so, since the small doorbell whose purpose was to announce any visitors was missing its clapper) where he was immediately welcomed by the warmth from the blazing fire in the stove. Fred had to smile as he remembered an earlier, darker time when the establishment was kept as cold as a crypt at the insistence of its proprietor, his uncle, Ebenezer Scrooge. Seven years ago, Scrooge was renowned as the coldest man in London, if not the world. It was said that his very touch could kill a flower, turning it into an icicle. Then at the age of fifty-three (but in appearance as ancient and stony as a gargoyle on a cathedral) he underwent a miraculous conversion that Fred was unable to explain to this day, retiring to bed on Christmas Eve a heartless miser who spread his misery like winter cold, and awakening the next morning a beam of sunshine, gleefully becoming a benefactor to the poor and the needy of the city, which were, unfortunately, legion. It was Fred Billings' belief that his uncle's former employee, and now his business partner, Bob Cratchit knew what meteor of joy had suddenly fallen from the heavens and struck the old man on the head, but he never revealed it, and Fred was forced to respect his reticence. Perhaps someday he would learn.

Festoons of gay holiday ribbons and wreaths adorned the walls of the counting house and draped over its shelves. Sprigs of holly were affixed to the doors of the two small private offices that were set back from the public area, one of which was presently dark and empty. In one corner of the office a gangly youth sat perched atop a tall stool and hunched over a clerk's desk, remaining oblivious to Fred's entrance.

The sight of the young man made Fred smile. A noble attempt had clearly been made to tame the young clerk's thick, carrot-colored hair, but the battle had been lost and the thatch remained as wild and uncontrollable as a tiger. The young man's face was dotted with freckles and his body was definitely at odds with his suit of clothing, with his bony knees and elbows threatening to poke holes in the material. Quill in hand, he pored over a ledger book, stopping every few seconds to count out a problem on his long fingers, the solution to which he recorded in the book quickly, before it got away.

"You are indeed a credit to your profession, Master Daniel," Fred said, though it took several seconds before the boy looked up. It was not that Daniel Cratchit was in any way slow of wit; rather, it was that the eighteen-year-old habitually became so engrossed in his duties that the world around him faded away. Finally his shaggy orange head lifted and he looked at Fred, his freckled face bursting into a broad grin. "Is that you, Mr. Billings, sir?" Daniel Cratchit cried.

"It is, Daniel," Fred said, holding out his hand. "How are you?"

"Well, sir, quite well," Daniel said, dropping his pen and sliding awkwardly off his stool in order to clasp Fred's hand and shake it heartily. "It is good to see you again, sir."

"My goodness, you have grown! You were just a lad the last time I saw you. Now you are nearly as tall as I."

"Taller than father," the boy said, proudly, although at least one inch of that pride was hair.

"And your position is suiting you?" Fred went on.

"Yes," Daniel answered tentatively, "though there is so very much to learn. I sometimes have a hard time retaining it all."

"I am certain you will succeed admirably," Fred said. "Your brother Tim; is he well?" Fred knew that the youngest of the Cratchit children, the boy who had once been called "Tiny Tim," had suffered another serious illness a few years ago and that his health at the best of times remained delicate.

"He is doing quite well indeed, Mr. Billings," Daniel replied, "at least as near as anyone can tell. You know Tim; he has never been one to complain about his condition, even when he is severely distressed."

From behind them, another voice chimed in: "Fred, how good it is to see you!" Fred Billings looked back to see the compact form of Daniel's father, Bob Cratchit, who rushed over to shake Fred's hand vigorously with both of his. "Thank you for coming so promptly."

"I came as soon as I received your letter," Fred replied, recognizing how, in the intervening years since he had seen his uncle's business partner, the man's hair had become streaked with silver and his girth had grown from spare to the first stage of portly. But nothing had diminished the warmth and kindness that were reflected in his eyes, which shone like candle lights in a wreath. "What is it that is so important you asked me to travel here in all haste?"

"Come into my office, and I will tell you all about it," Bob Cratchit responded, a look of concern darkening his hearty face. "Daniel, please take Mr. Billings' hat and coat and set them by the fire to dry, would you? Not too close, mind you; we do not want to burn a guest's clothing…again."

With difficulty, Fred stifled a laugh.

The office of Bob Cratchit was not large, but it was tidy and comfortable. After closing the door, Bob seated himself behind his desk…at least what Fred assumed was his desk, being so thoroughly buried under heaps of papers and ledgers that positive identification was all but impossible. Taking a chair at Bob's request, Fred remarked: "Your son is a fine boy, if I am any judge."

"Oh, Daniel is the salt of the earth," Bob replied. "I am a lucky man, Fred. All of my children have been a credit to me. Martha has her own milliner's shop now and Peter has embarked on a career as a writer."

"Indeed?"

"Yes, my attempts to tie Peter to an apprentice's stool proved to be quite hopeless. And our Belinda was wed last year to a fine man who owns an estate in Surrey."

"Daniel mentioned that Tim is well."

Bob Cratchit's face took on a faraway look. "Tim remains a marvel, Fred. A marvel encased in an enigma. Sometimes I wonder if it is not he who is the father and I the son. When my good wife died two years ago, I do not think I could have made it through the ordeal without Tim at my side. I should have been comforting him, for it was he who lost his mother. But instead he comforted me. God alone knows where that boy gets his strength and wisdom." Cratchit's eyes became watery as they looked off in the distance. A moment later, he shook himself out of it. "But I did not ask you to rush to London to discuss familial matters. The situation at hand involves your uncle."

"I rather feared as much," Fred said. "Is Uncle Ebenezer ill?"

"Physically, no," Bob replied. "At least I don't think so. He has not complained of any illness, except for those afflictions that would be expected in a man of his years. But he has fallen into a great gloom, a despair of some sort, which is very peculiar for a man who of late has been the very soul of cheerfulness."

"Perhaps it is the fog," Fred suggested. "I could not help but notice that the people I passed on the streets were in a similar sort of mood."

"I have noticed that as well. It is like the entire city has sunk into a darkness of spirit. But it appears to be much worse with your uncle. He has been arriving late at the office, if he bothers to come in at all, and it is a chore to get so much as a 'good morning' out of him. Then he goes into his private office, shuts the door, and sits in brooding silence until the middle of the afternoon, at which time he leaves without a word. It is like working with the shade of a man."

Fred leaned forward in his chair. "How long has this been going on?"

"For a fortnight, at least, although over the last several days it has gotten worse. The most troubling sign came last week when Tim came by to see him, an event that usually lifts his spirits immeasurably. This time, however, he closed his office door and refused to see him. He would not come out until Tim had gone, which upset Tim greatly."

"And Uncle gave no reason for this behavior?"

"None whatsoever. He left the office that evening without so much as a word to either Daniel or I and I have not seen him since. Yesterday I attempted to visit him at his house. I was allowed entry by one of his tenants, a young boy named Joby who is admirable in manners, but less so in cleanliness, but when I went upstairs and knocked upon the door of his rooms, he refused to open it."

Fred Billing's face darkened with concern. "Should we be seeking out a physician?"

"I do not know," Bob replied, shaking his head. "As I have said, I do not believe his affliction to have a physical cause, and even if we were to summon a doctor, I don't know that he would allow him into his rooms. He appears more troubled of spirit and mind than of body. After his rejection of Tim, as he was preparing to leave for the evening, I sought him out to discuss the placement of the Christmas decorations and the amounts of our traditional charity gifts. It is a subject to which he normally warms like a fire, yet this time he reacted as though he had tasted poison. 'Don't speak to me of Christmas,' were his exact words."

"Dear heavens," Fred cried, "you don't think Uncle is reverting to his old ways do you?"

"I truly hope not," Bob said, "but I cannot explain his manner in any other way. That is why I summoned you here. You and I were among the first beneficiaries of his change of heart seven years ago. Therefore I believe it is our duty to discover what is causing him to change back, if that is what is taking place, and try to help him however we can."

Rising from his chair, Fred Billings declared: "Then I shall go to him at once. I will tell him that my own business brought me into London, and that I could not leave the city again in good conscience without first having seen him. I'll say that I stopped around here first, and finding him absent——"

"No, Fred, I think it would be best if you did not mention coming here, or talking to me first."

"Why not?"

Bob rose and stepped around the overburdened desk. "Because I remember his previous personality only too well, that overwhelming mistrust of people he used to possess, particularly those he believed wanted something from him. We should do nothing that might rekindle that sense of mistrust, or exacerbate it if it has already been

10

resurrected. If he were to learn that you and I had been meeting regarding his welfare, he might regard it as a conspiracy against him and react in a way befitting the old Mr. Scrooge."

"I understand. Leave it to me, Bob, I will find some way to break through to him."

"If anyone can do it, Fred, it is you."

After making his farewell to Bob Cratchit, Fred Billings stepped back into the waiting room of the counting house to retrieve his now warmed greatcoat from the care of Daniel, and after a hearty goodbye to the young man he took leave of the establishment of Scrooge and Cratchit.

St. Michael's Alley now seemed even darker and colder than before, as though the entire district of the city were under a great shadow. As he strode down the street, taking in the sights of the city he loved, no matter how obscured by fog and gloom they were, one figure in particular caught Fred's attention. Standing on the opposite side of the narrow street was a very tall man in a flared hat, whose clothes were of the best cut. He carried himself with the bearing of a gentleman, but that is not what caused Fred to stop and study the tall figure. It was instead because the man was staring directly at him.

Do I know that fellow? Fred wondered, as the man on the other side of the street continued to study him, up and down. Even at this distance, Fred could feel the man's gaze boring into him, examining him like a lepidopterist studies a dead butterfly pinned to a board. Then the man suddenly turned away and began to retreat.

"Hold, sir!" Fred called out, but the tall man made no attempt to answer. "Wait up, please!" Fred shouted again, stepping into the muddy street to cross it. A coach led by a full team of horses clopped in front of him, momentarily obscuring his view of the fellow. By the time it had passed, the strange man was nowhere to be seen.

11

Fred Billings shuddered, and not entirely because of the chill weather. There was something about the demeanor of that solemn, staring figure——no, not simply something; *everything*——that had unnerved Fred in a way that no other person ever had. He hoped that his Uncle Ebenezer had a fire in his hearth when he arrived at his house, because he felt as though he would need it. In his entire life, he could not recall ever feeling such a sensation of dark, desolate coldness.

As Fred made his way to the home of his uncle, which was but a few streets away, he was all but overcome by an alien sense of despair that seemed to fall on him like bitter rain.

TWO

The house of Ebenezer Scrooge, which had previously belonged to his one-time partner Jacob Marley, bore a façade that was as craggy and weather-beaten as an old sailor's face. Four families called this structure their home, each inhabiting a comfortable set of rooms separate from those of its owner. On any given day, regardless of the season, the sounds of frolicking children could be heard within its walls and the smells of cooking could be detected. The families were asked to pay in rent each month two shillings, a paltry sum that each tenant considered an example of the great generosity of their landlord, Ebenezer Scrooge, but which Scrooge himself considered part of his duty to the cause of humanity.

Scrooge's chambers were on the house's first floor, up a staircase so wide that a full coach-and-four could easily ascend it. Its furnishings remained as plain as in the days when he had been widely known as a miser. In that earlier time he had refused to spend more on his surroundings than was absolutely essential, so as not to deplete his wealth. Now he believed it was more important to use his wealth to help others rather than to cater to his own situation.

At this moment, however, his furnishings were the furthest things from Ebenezer Scrooge's mind. He sat morosely in his chair by the fireplace, staring absently into the dancing flames and stroking his fat, languid calico cat Fanny, who was curled, warm and purring, on his lap. He had not moved from this position since the morning, having remained in his bedclothes and robe for the entire day, brooding about life and about age, but most of all, about failure.

His failure.

Not that his business was failing. His decision to make Bob Cratchit a full partner had resulted in his business becoming twice as successful. Neither was he a failure in the eyes of the many people who greeted him on the street most normal days, nor those whom he knew personally. Among the city, he was known as "The Benefactor of London"…which made his failure even more painful to bear.

Ebenezer Scrooge felt a failure to himself.

He amongst men had been given a second chance at life, a chance at redemption, and an opportunity to change the world around him. His late partner Marley——the most unlikely of saviors——and three subsequent ghosts had shown him the folly and misery of his ways, and fostered a desire to do good for others; and he had striven to do so, striven with his every ounce of being. For seven years Scrooge had done everything he could think of to procure the betterment of his fellow Londoners, not simply to erase his former image as a heartless wretch, but out of a genuine concern to make up for lost time and help as many men, women, and children as was possible. He had given away a lifetime's worth of wealth; he had worked tirelessly on behalf of the downtrodden and unfortunate classes; he had even opened his home to poor families. But what had been the ultimate result of all his time and philanthropy?

Nothing.

Despite everything he had done, poverty not only remained a constant in the city, it increased. Hunger was everywhere. Disease was rampant. Children continued to be exploited in workhouses. The society of London was more alive with misery than it had ever been. For all the good he had been able to impart in these last seven years, he might as well have never been visited by the spirits. For all of the lasting change he had enacted, he might as well have been struck dead that night rather than undergoing a reformation.

From somewhere, he could hear the god of misery laughing at his folly.

Scrooge's heart was as heavy as coal as he continued to sit and brood, his head slowly shaking back and forth, as though buffeted by the futility of existence. Only the light, rhythmic knocking on the door of his suite interrupted his flame-borne trance. Fanny slowly lifted her orange and white head towards the sound, opening one sleepy eye. The other eye opened at the second knock, after which Scrooge called out, "The door is unlocked, Joby."

Joby Partle, a boy of eight whose family lived on the floor below, and who wore his weeks' worth of dirt as proudly as a Punjab medal, poked his head inside. "'Owd'jer know it was me?" the boy asked.

Still cradling the cat in his arms, Scrooge rose from the chair stiffly and walked toward the door. "I knew it was you, Joby, for the simple reason that no one else has a cause to call on me. So, let me guess why you are here. No doubt you've come snooping around hoping to pick up another ha'penny, is that it?" Scrooge often hired the boy to perform odd tasks or run errands for him, and he usually enjoyed the boy's company. But today Joby's sudden appearance only deepened his black mood. "Well, speak up!"

"N-no sir," Joby said, startled by his "uncle's" brusque manner. "Me mum thought maybe you was sick or somethin', that's all. She hasn't seen you lately, so she sent me up t'check. I didn't mean nothin'."

The hurt expression on the urchin's face cut through Scrooge's heavy heart. Handing Fanny to the boy, who accepted the purring creature with affection, he said: "Please forgive me, Joby, I had no cause to speak to you like that. I'm afraid I have been feeling poorly of late, and that caused me to speak in an unkind and harsh way. I am sorry."

"It's all right, Mr. Scrooge," Joby muttered. "Is there anything I can do to 'elp?"

"You're a fine lad, Master Partle," Scrooge said, ruffling Joby's thick dark hair, which drew from the boy a broad smile. "Since you are here, there is a task you could accomplish for me."

"Yes sir?"

Walking to the mantelpiece, Scrooge picked up a battered tin cup and from it fished out a coin. "Please go to my place of business and inform Mr. Cratchit that I do not expect to come in tomorrow."

"An' the day after that, no one'll be there," the boy said cheerfully. When Scrooge looked at him wonderingly, Joby shouted: "It's Christmas!"

"Oh, yes, of course." Scrooge deftly flipped the coin into the air (for no matter how infirm the rest of body became, his fingers retained their dexterity for manipulating money), and Joby, equally deftly, caught it, his eyes widening.

"A whole tuppence?"

"Consider it a Christmas gift. Now go on, Joby, be about it."

"Yes sir!" Joby said. "And Merry Christmas, Mr. Scrooge!" The boy dashed out of the room, forgetting to set down the cat. Returning, he placed her on the floor and then ran out again, closing the door behind him.

Stepping to the window that overlooked the street, Scrooge watched as Joby tore through the gloom, leaping over puddles and darting in and out between moving hansom cabs, dodging people and horses alike. Even after the boy had disappeared into the grey mist, Scrooge continued to watch the street with sharp eyes that were miraculously undimmed by age. What he saw was not the

16

London of commerce and progress, of pomp and ceremony, of history and dignity. This was the secret heart of London, where life was lived at all levels, where the horses that pulled the drays through the muddy streets often ate better than the ragged men and women who darted out of their paths.

The late afternoon drizzle was heavier now. As the near-freezing rain fell, the people of the city either retreated inside or sheltered themselves as best they could in doorways. As the street under Scrooge's window began to clear, one figure came into view: A young woman, little more than a girl, who walked with a strange, hopping gait as she made her way across the street. The thinness of her dress and shawl was scant protection against the frigid weather, and soon Scrooge saw the reason for her peculiar walk: the girl was barefoot.

She carried a bundle with her, the contents of which Scrooge could not make out. Dashing through the wet street, she stopped again on the walk in front of his house.

There was movement in the bundle she carried.

"A dog?" Scrooge said to no one.

The girl——for now he could clearly see that she was no more than twelve years old——held out one hand to the people who passed by, while clutching the squirming bundle with the other. No one stopped to help her; no one even deigned to look at the pathetic girl as they walked past. "Help her, someone, for God's sake," Scrooge uttered, unable to take his eyes off the terrible drama on the street below. Still no one stopped...until one man, elegantly dressed in a tall hat and great coat, and carrying a walking stick came to a halt in front of her.

"Yes," Scrooge hissed.

After surveying the girl up and down, the man took his stick and dashed her to the ground, and continued to walk.

"Damn you!" Scrooge cried out, his hot breath steaming the inside of the window's cold glass.

Wiping away the condensation, he watched as the girl returned to her feet and desperately began to search for her bundle, which she had dropped when struck. Scrooge saw her find the cloth, and then find something else — the object that was wrapped inside.

It was a baby. A naked, blue boy that was now wailing against the cold, the rain, and hunger with such force that it penetrated every wall of the house, as well as every corner of his mind. Turning, he raced as best he could to the coin cup on his mantle and overturned it into his hands. Then he dashed back and struggled to unlatch the window. Finally pushing it open, he leaned out as far as he dared, ignoring the stinging, cold pelting on his face and chest. "Here!" he cried, holding out his coin-stuffed fist. "Take it, get food, get shelter!"

Scrooge dropped the money into the street, watching the circles of silver and gold plop onto the sidewalk like miraculous rain. But his eyes were so clouded by tears, which were now on the verge of freezing, that he could not see the street clearly. When the saline cloud over his vision lifted, he was able to gaze down on the street again.

The girl and the baby were now gone. Instead, a gathering of men and women, many of whom were dressed in finery better than his own wardrobe, were bent over and scrambling to pick up the coins. One man pushed aside a much younger boy in order to grasp the last shilling for himself. Within moments, the small, greedy crowd had dispersed with some laughing and cheering their literal windfall as they continued down the street.

What had happened to the girl and the infant? Perhaps somebody had indeed stopped to help them while he had taken his eyes off of her. Perhaps through the kindness of some soul they were finally being escorted to warmth and safety.

Perhaps…but he knew better. This was London.

Scrooge dropped to knees, his head nearly scraping the worn floorboards of his bedroom.

"Damn you!" Scrooge again wailed, this time to the city. "Damn you to Hell. And damn me, too."

Too late, the old man thought. *Always too late. That is my curse. I was not redeemed by Jacob Marley, all those years ago, I was cursed by him...cursed to fail.*

Fanny the cat padded her way towards him and placed a tentative paw on his lap, but Scrooge was hardly aware of her presence. A dull, empty ache in his chest hindered his breath. Struggling to his feet, he swung the casing window closed and re-latched it, then staggered to his bed and fell hopelessly onto the mattress, praying for sleep, for oblivion, for something to take him away from his mortal failure.

Yet sleep refused to come; release from dread was replaced by the awareness of a mysterious fog that lapped slowly at the edges of the bed. Scrooge became aware of an odor permeating the room——it was unmistakably the smell of cold earth. The room was now bathed in an otherworldly glow, and his bed curtains billowed from an unnatural breeze.

"Is someone there?" Scrooge asked in a frightened voice, but received no answer.

Getting out of the bed, he moved through the room which was now filled with a greenish mist. Suddenly thirsty, Scrooge moved to the small dresser that was set against one wall, on which sat a water ewer and wash basin, and a large oval mirror. Glancing into it as he poured the water into a glass, he saw himself as he was: an old, wizened, dark-eyed man whose face bore the travails of his life. He did not look well. But in the next second, his face began to change, becoming sterner and more unpleasant. A cruel grimace marred his mouth, and his eyes seemed to glow, but with a cold darkness.

19

"What is happening?" Scrooge asked, but his lips did not move in his mirror reflection. "Oh, dear Lord," he uttered as he fully recognized the figure in the mirror; it was him, and yet it was not...at least not the Ebenezer Scrooge who had walked London for the past seven years. The figure in the mirror was the *old* Scrooge, the one who had "died" after his evening with the spirits...or so he prayed.

"I wished never to see you again," Scrooge said.

"Yet here I am," his doppelganger replied in a harsh voice. "You have summoned me."

"Nonsense! I have no use for you whatsoever! Why should I call you forth?"

"Why indeed," his dark twin said. In the next instant it faded from the mirror, only to reappear in the reflection standing behind him! Whirling around, Scrooge confronted the figure, whose suit of clothing now appeared dusty and old, as though having been kept locked up in a storage closet for years.

"This cannot be," Scrooge said. "You were killed seven years ago."

"I do not kill so easily."

"But why have you returned? Why do you haunt me now?"

"I have haunted you for years," the dark twin sneered. "I haunt you the way all men's pasts haunt them. I am the man you were. I embody the acts you performed, the words you spoke, even the thoughts in your head. They are what propel my existence. They are...*I am*...still a part of you. Fools continue to strive to change the future all the while ignoring the truth that they cannot change the past; *nothing* can change the past. It is set as stone and incapable of eroding."

"Still, there remains the future," Scrooge argued.

"That is nothing more than a chimera, one which remains as unknown to man as ever," the doppelganger intoned. "The past, however, is forged in iron. There is only the present, and what is that? It is misery, poverty, pain, degradation, even for children. Especially for those children who have little past and will know no future, but only suffer the ordeal of the present. That has not changed. *You* have not changed."

Bitterness rose in Scrooge's gorge like an illness. "Be gone, I beg of you," he whimpered, hot tears emerging once more from Ebenezer Scrooge's eyes.

"Ah, the drops of despair," the twin continued. "It is that very despair that has summoned me. Soon we will be together again as one."

"NO!" Scrooge shouted, forcefully. "I reject that! I have lived up to my promise, I tell you! I have done my very best!"

"Yet it was hardly enough. You have striven to make the world better yet you have done nothing. You have failed miserably, which you acknowledge yourself. When you and I were one, you were *something*, Scrooge; a man of business, of prosperity. A man no one called a fool. Now you are the biggest fool in London, a pathetic failure who is laughed at and scorned by everyone he passes on the street. You may not hear their laughter, their ridicule, but I do."

Scrooge buried his face in his hands. "Please stop, for the love of God," he moaned. "Leave me in peace."

"Peace is what I have come to offer," the doppelganger said. "As well as the alleviation of pain, of heartache, of despair."

"How?"

The dark spirit pointed a bony finger toward the window, which unlatched itself and once more opened outward, letting the freezing, dank night inside. "That night seven years ago I stepped out of that window and journeyed over the city, over the ocean, into the past and into the vision of the future…a false vision, as it has proven, since it did not predict your utter failure. Now we shall do it together. Come, Scrooge; take my hand. Step to the window."

"Wh...what will happen if I do?"

"All of your problems will end in an instant. No more pain, no more despair, no more human suffering. We will be one again...for eternity."

"You cannot force me to take my life!" Scrooge cried.

After a long silence, the dark twin said, "You are right, I cannot. That is a choice only you can make. But consider what you would be preserving by *not* coming with me. Misery, failure, endless frustration as your body continues to weaken with age, until you are nothing but a ruined husk of a man consumed by the truth that you were unable to make a single positive change in the human condition. How many more months can your mind and body withstand that? You have the choice to end your suffering here and now."

A dull ache formed in Ebenezer Scrooge's chest. Ending his torment would indeed be easy. When his body was found on the street it would be assumed he had fallen accidentally. No one would know of his ultimate failure...the failure of life. "End it," he panted. "I can end it."

"Your decision now will make the difference between release and a continued lifetime of anguish," the horrible spirit goaded.

Scrooge took a step toward the window, unable to think about anything except assuaging his agony, both that in his chest, which was intensifying, and that of his spirit. The ghost of the man he had previously been spoke the truth: had lived too long and done too little. Maybe if he had not thrown so much of his life away before experiencing redemption, the story would be different, but the past could not be changed. His entire life had been one long, wretched failure.

He was standing in front of the window now, looking out onto the bitterly cold and wet night. His heart pounded audibly as he reached out for the hand of his dark twin and raised a foot, placing it onto the window sill.

"You are making the correct decision, Scrooge," his other told him. "Only one step and your travails are over."

Scrooge put his other hand against the casement jamb of the window to support himself as he stood on the sill, crouched by the low lintel. He moved one foot and held it over the street far below.

"We are one now," his double whispered.

But before Scrooge could complete what would have been his last act in life, a new sound was heard in his bedroom, one that drove away the terrible, gloating voice. It was a long, loud wail of horror. Scrooge's head snapped back as he teetered on the damp window sill. Then he identified the source of the noise: it was his Fanny, his calico cat, who threw herself at him and wrapped herself around his leg.

Taking his hand off of the window frame, Scrooge fell backward into the room, landing hurtfully on his bony rump...in pain, but alive. His doppelganger was nowhere to be seen now, and the eerie green miasma that had permeated the room had similarly vanished.

"Are you all right, Fanny?" Scrooge cried, and a second later the cat leapt into his arms, proving that she was. "Oh, my dear Lord, Fanny, what would have become of you if I had been so foolish as to give in to my worst impulse?"

He held her long enough for her terror to give way to contented purring, and then gently placed her on the floor, while struggling to his feet. Icy wind continued to blow into the bedroom from the open window. "Enough of that," he said, going to it to latch it closed again. But in the course of reaching out to grasp the handle of the window, Ebenezer Scrooge lost his balance.

"No!" he cried as he fell through the opening.

Scrooge continued to fall, expecting at any moment to feel his body slam onto the street below…but that sensation never came. He continued to fall, long after she should have landed, tumbling uncontrollably through nothingness, until blackness overtook him.

THREE

Slowly and apprehensively, Ebenezer Scrooge opened his eyes. He was lying on a cold, hard surface with no memory of landing. The blackness was gone, yet shadows remained. The toll of a clock striking midnight was heard. Where he was at that moment he could not say, except that it was a place that felt familiar, yet strangely foreign. Rising to a sitting position, he quickly discovered that he was now completely dressed in his best suit, embroidered waistcoat, cravat and thick stockings. In his last memory, that of falling through the window of his room, he had been wearing nothing more than his bedclothes, a robe, and a nightcap. How could he suddenly be dressed?

Had he switched places with the horrible, goading ghost of his former self?

"Welcome, Ebenezer Scrooge," said a warming, musical voice reminiscent of chimes sounding in a gentle breeze.

Startled, Scrooge sat up, his eyes battling the darkness around him in hopes of identifying the speaker. "Who is there?"

"A friend, here to congratulate you."

"Congratulate me for what?"

"For making the right choice." He was able to make out the shimmering figure of a young woman dressed in a robe the color of snow, which was cinched around her waist by a green wreath. Her long, silken hair was of the same snowy white, so white, in fact, that it seemed to melt into her robe and meld with it where it fell upon the cloth. A single sprig of holly adorned the top of her head, though the green of the leaves could in no way compare to the deep, pure emerald of her eyes, which were the most crystalline Scrooge had ever seen. Her face, which was the color and texture of bone china, strangely possessed the characteristics of both a child and an adult, not in conflict with one another, but somehow living harmoniously in a lovely union. Only the red shadows under each eye, signs of worry, stood as flaws in the perfection of her face.

"Who are you?" Scrooge asked, struck by her beauty.

"You may call me Carillon," she answered.

Scrooge rose to his feet, his back and knees complaining from the exertion. "That is your name?"

She smiled sweetly. "It is what you may call me."

Scrooge shook his head and sighed. Clearly he was being visited by a spirit of some sort, and he knew from experience, more so than most mortals, that those of the other world rarely gave simple, understandable answers. "Where am I?" he asked, "and how did I become dressed thusly? I do not remember doing so."

"You will need to look presentable when you arrive at your destination, Ebenezer Scrooge," the glowing figure replied. "Bedclothes are inappropriate."

"I…I fell from my window."

"You did, by accident. You no longer held the intention of doing so, and because of that we were able to catch you. Had you instead chosen to take your own life deliberately, we would have been powerless to help."

While that was hardly an explanation, Scrooge sensed that pursuing the matter further would never result in a better one. "Who are *we*, Carillon, and what is this destination you speak of?" Scrooge asked.

"Follow me," the lovely young spirit said, and he did. Leaving the strange room in which he had awakened, Scrooge soon found himself in a tunnel-like stone corridor.

He froze. Carillon stopped walking as well. "What is it, Ebenezer Scrooge?" she asked.

You correctly said that I decided against taking my own life at the last moment, yet I did indeed suffer a fall. Now I am on my way to a 'destination' and dressed as though for my own funeral! Tell me...am I dead? Are you leading me to Hell?"

Carillon began to laugh, a sound that was like a choir of bells. "No, Ebenezer Scrooge, you are not dead, and as for Hell, Man makes his own Hell, and your life has been such that I daresay you have managed to escape that fate."

Can you be certain of this? Scrooge thought grimly.

"Please, Ebenezer Scrooge, we must hurry." She held out her hand to him and Scrooge took it reluctantly. Even though he knew from experience that the spirits could be trusted, he nevertheless faced this new visitation with apprehension. Was he to be sent on yet another night journey, like the one seven years ago? If so, to what end?

The touch of Carillon's delicate fingers felt like gently falling snow. Utilizing her glowing aura, the spirit led Scrooge down what appeared to be a dark hallway carved out of stone. "Will you not tell me where we are going?" he asked.

"All will be answered when we arrive," Carillon responded.

There were countless questions rushing through Ebenezer Scrooge's mind as they continued through the strange hallway, so many that he was unable to formulate any one of them into a coherent query. Before he even had a chance to try, they arrived at an enormous wooden door supported by ancient iron hinges that were set into the end of the stone passageway. A huge brass ring was affixed to it; lifting it, Carillon pushed on the door, which slowly opened with an ominous creak.

On the other side was a dimly lit, cavernous chamber whose walls were covered with threadbare and dusty tapestries into which were woven images of dancing and festivities, though even the figures depicted in the tapestries appeared tired and heavy-laden. Placed sparsely throughout were crumbling pieces of furniture that appeared unfit for use. The overall appearance was that of a chamber that had not been entered for years. Yet it looked as though it had long ago been set for a grand celebration. Hanging from the rafters were boughs and branches, once green, now bare. Dead sprigs of holly sporting hard, blackened berries were twisted into grim wreaths that were held together by tatters of faded, dusty ribbon. Shriveled ivy hung down limply from a beam in the center of the room, and in one corner stood a once-full fir tree, nearly twice as tall as Scrooge, its barren branches sporting a few broken glass ornaments and burnt candles. Scattered underneath it were a handful of demolished toys: a headless doll, a broken drum, a sled with rusted and bent runners, and a tiny dollhouse that sat in ruins. In one wall was an enormous fireplace, the mantle as high as a man, and in it was a single smoldering log, set upright. As Scrooge approached it, he detected a strange, faint mixture of odors, including incense and pine, wassail and mince, roast goose and stuffing, all of which combined to produce one special scent. It was unmistakably the aroma of Christmas...yet it seemed somehow fouled.

"What has happened?" Scrooge asked.

Instead of answering, Carillon simply looked towards a large dining table with places for many guests, which sat in the center of the room. It was set for a feast, but one of which no person would willingly partake. In the center of the table on a tarnished tray sat a wizened, scrawny goose, its stuffing sodden and moldy. Bowls of shriveled vegetables surrounded it, and at one end of the table was a fallen pudding. Several goblets held old wine that reeked of vinegar.

Heaped in yet another corner of the room were broken and dusty musical instruments. If there were such a thing as a room that had died, Scrooge thought, this was it. "What place is this?" he asked.

"This is the House of Yuletide," Carillon answered, a tone of sadness weighing down her light voice. "At least it was. Come."

Following her through yet another large vaulted door, Scrooge entered a chamber that was somewhat similar to his own bedroom, but lacking in windows of any kind. Against one wall was an enormous bed, and in it, faintly illuminated by flickering candles, was a man. The figure was pathetically wasted, little more than a living skeleton, though the folds of loose and hanging flesh implied that once the man was of a formidable size. The face, while drawn and sallow, still betrayed noble features, and wisps of dark brown hair could still be detected in the sparse white beard. Scrooge regarded the poor soul with great sadness and pity, but the horrible realization of the figure's identity did not dawn on him until he took closer notice of his pine-green robe with fur trim——once as fine as a king's raiment, but now ratty and worn——and the wreath of brittle dead holly leaves that fell down around his withered brow.

The figure opened its rheumy eyes and a sick parody of a smile stretched his cracked lips. "Look upon me, Scrooge," he moaned. "You have, alas, seen the likes of me before."

The words drove into Scrooge's brain like spikes. He had heard them once before, when the figure's voice had been robust and jovial. "It cannot be!" he cried.

"It is," Carillon replied, sadly

Moving in closer to the figure in the bed, Scrooge's foot knocked against an extinguished torch that lay on the floor, and at once he knew it as the property of the figure in the bed, the boisterous giant he had met seven years ago, who had transported him to witness the celebrations being prepared by his nephew Fred and Bob Cratchit, both of whom could ill afford them.

29

"*The Ghost of Christmas Present*," Ebenezer Scrooge uttered in horror, and the once roaring, now wasted figure closed his eyes and nodded. It was he; and yet it was not he. At least it was not the spirit Scrooge had encountered all those years ago, not in form. "You are not as I remember you."

"You not remember me at all," the gaunt figure said weakly. "It was my brother whom you encountered seven years ago. The essence of you is embedded in my consciousness, however, as it was for my last six elder brothers." The Ghost of Christmas Present was stricken with a racking cough after which his head fell back onto the faded pillow. His body became still; its only movement was its slow, labored breathing. Carillon led Scrooge away from the bed.

"What is wrong with him?" he asked.

"He is dying," the spirit replied.

"How is it possible for a spirit to die?"

"Spirits are far more vulnerable than humans, Ebenezer Scrooge. The Ghost of Christmas Present fades away at midnight every December the twenty-fifth, and is reborn in kind the following December, and so the cycle has continued for tens of centuries. This one, though, was born sickly and he has grown even worse with each passing hour." Carillon looked at Scrooge with imploring eyes. "You must help him."

"Help him? My dear, what possible service could I offer?"

"One greater than you can imagine," she replied, leading Scrooge though another large door and into a paneled room that contained an overstuffed chair and a hearth with a meager fire, to which Scrooge rushed in order to warm his hands.

"I never used to feel cold, you know," he told the spirit. "Throughout most of my life I was impervious to it. Now it seems I cannot get enough warmth. If you were to move our sickly friend into this room, perchance he would recover."

"It is Darkness, not coldness, that afflicts him," Carillon said. "If the Darkness continues to encroach, he will not survive to Christmas Day. He must not be allowed to die, Ebenezer Scrooge. You are the only one who can save him."

"Child, I am not a medical man. I know nothing of healing."

"Yet a boy who had been given up for lost lives today because of you."

"It was not I who restored Tim Cratchit to health. It was a physician. I had little to do with it."

"On the contrary, Ebenezer Scrooge, you had everything to do with it, for you believed in your heart that it could be done, and so set about to make it so. That is what is required to save the Ghost of Christmas."

"I do not understand you."

"Belief, Ebenezer Scrooge. Belief is what is required."

"Belief in what?"

"In him. In the very spirit of Christmas. He is dying because he is no longer wanted. Christmas is no longer wanted."

"Not wanted? Humbug!"

"If only it were a humbug. "The Balance is tipping, Ebenezer Scrooge. It is tipping at an alarming rate."

Scrooge's head was beginning to throb. "The balance is tipping," he repeated, rubbing his temples with his bony fingers in an attempt to drive the growing pain away. "What is this balance?"

"You have remained ignorant of the forces that governed your spiritual journey some years back because there was no need to inform you of them," Carillon said. "There is now. I will endeavor to explain it to you, though I must do so quickly, as we have little time. Please sit down, Ebenezer Scrooge."

31

Scrooge seated himself in the chair near the hearth.

"The world as you know it is ruled by two influences," the spirit began. "One side offers joy, hope, compassion and generosity while the other promotes the basest elements of human nature: despair, hopelessness, corruption, selfishness and deliberate evil. Since the beginning of time there has been equipoise between these two forces, which are constantly engaged in battle for dominion over humankind. Throughout the ages the forces of Light have changed, altered, and been adapted to best reflect the current needs of believers, but the essence of the Light has remained constant. The Darkness, however, never changes. Many times one side or the other, either the Light or the Darkness, has gained temporary sovereignty over the world, only to relinquish it to the other side at a later time. But it is established within the Great Order of the world that one side shall never completely vanquish the other. That is known as the Balance."

"So all the good in the world is offset by evil," Scrooge considered.

"Is that so surprising?"

"Not at all. But would it not be more beneficial if the side of good were to overcome the side of darkness forever?"

"The side of Darkness has too many adherents for that to occur."

Carillon did not continue the thought in words, but Scrooge was somehow able to read it on her face. "But it is *possible* for the side of the Light to be vanquished?"

"It is," she admitted. "We have always had the harder struggle."

Now Scrooge's head felt like it was about to burst. "You keep using the term *we*," he said. "Are you simply referring to the adherents of Light?"

"I am specifically referring to those like me," she said, "the Warriors of Helios. We serve the side of Light. We

32

carry out the battle against the Warriors of Stygios, those who cater to the side of Darkness. Warriors on each side are abetted by *travelers*, mortals who may or may not be aware of their conscription into the battle itself...mortals such as you, Ebenezer Scrooge."

Scrooge's mind was racing like a runaway dray. "So the very order of the world is maintained essentially by press gangs for good and evil?" he asked.

The spirit smiled. "If that way of looking at it helps you understand the situation, then it is an accurate statement."

"Am I correct in assuming that I was once abetting the side of Darkness, but since my reformation I have thrown my allegiance to the side of Light?"

"You are. Within every mortal resides the power to choose between Light and Darkness. You demonstrated that this very evening. Some are born into the Light and gain awareness of their roles at a certain stage of life. Young Timothy Cratchit, for example."

"Tiny Tim?"

"Had he died those seven years ago, the Light would have lost one of its most powerful travelers. Others, such as you, Ebenezer Scrooge, follow one path but then reverse themselves and follow the other."

Sitting near the faint warmth of the fireplace, Scrooge still felt himself becoming chilled as he recalled his visitation earlier that evening. "Somehow I appear to still be following both," he said. "I was haunted by the specter of my past tonight. How can he...I mean me...I mean what I used to be still exist?"

"You were a powerful traveler then, Ebenezer Scrooge, as you are now," Carillon told him. "The Dark energy you engendered in your earlier life does indeed remain, and the Lord of Stygios found a way to use it."

"Who is the Lord of Stygios?"

"Tenebra. It is he who commands the armies of the Darkness against us, most of whom do not even realize they are being so called. Had you done his bidding this evening and taken your life, you would have become his eternally-cursed servant, like Jacob Marley."

"*Marley*? No, spirit, that cannot be! It was old Marley who journeyed back from the grave to make me a different man!"

"Helios offered you the choice, but *you* made yourself a traveler for the Light. You could have refused to repent and reform after your experience with the spirits. You could have gone on as an unwitting minion of the side of Darkness. Yet you did not." The spirit fell silent for a moment, and her delicate face took on an expression of thoughtful deliberation. "Have you ever wondered why you were visited by so many spirits on that night? It was to fulfill the Balance. You see, Ebenezer Scrooge, you were then the subject of a wager."

"A wager? Whatever do you mean?"

"Any mortal who demonstrates an extreme capacity for change, one way or the other, attracts the attention of the sides of Light and Darkness. In your youth you were filled with goodness, yet with time you began to follow the path of the Darkness. That change was noticed by both sides. At the point when it appeared that the Darkness was to have you on their side forever, Pere Ivor, the Lord of Helios, issued a challenge to Lord Tenebra of the Darkness a wager: each side would send two emissaries to you and it would be up to you to choose the path of your ultimate allegiance. From the Light came the spirits you knew as the Ghosts of Christmas Past and Christmas Present— the Spirit of Christmas himself—while the Darkness sent the Ghost of Christmas Yet to Come and Jacob Marley, who was dispatched to issue you the challenge of facing the three spirits. Tenebra did not believe you would actually agree to face them. Had you rejected Jacob Marley as a nightmare brought upon by indigestion, the challenge would have ended, the wager would have been won, and the Darkness would have collected their spoils. But you chose to believe your eyes and ears, which Tenebra considered an act of betrayal. Even then, though, he was convinced of victory once you had encountered his second minion."

Ebenezer Scrooge shuddered as he remembered the third and most terrifying ghost: the black-robed, faceless, silent figure who pointed with bony fingers towards the grave bearing Scrooge's own name. The Ghost of Christmas Yet to Come had been the only spirit who would not talk to him or answer his questions. It showed him nothing but bleak hopelessness and misery. It showed him the chasm of death; his own and Tim Cratchit's.

"The mission of that spirit was simple, Ebenezer Scrooge," Carillon continued. "It was meant to scare you to *death*, unrepentant. But that did not happen."

Scrooge was shaking as he said: "I remember asking, nay, begging that horrible apparition to tell me if the sights he showed me were the things that must be, or only the things might be. It would not."

"It could not, for only you had the power to answer that question. That was the choice you were offered. When Tenebra lost the wager, not only was the Balance restored, but for a brief time it shifted slightly to the side of Light. It was a heavy loss for the Darkness, and a bitter one, and Tenebra has never forgotten it. The thirst for vengeance is what has driven him to expand the power of the Darkness to the point where it is nearly unstoppable. If the Darkness is allowed to overwhelm the Light, then it will hold permanent dominion over the earth."

"Good heavens," Scrooge uttered. "How can that transpire as long as this Balance you speak of exists? Is there no governing force overseeing it?"

"There is indeed a High Justice which sits in judgment over the Balance."

"Very well, then! He...or it...or whatever will prevent this Tenebra creature from prevailing."

The spirit's beautiful face fell in sadness. "Like your earthly judges of court, the High Justice hears the arguments of Humankind as presented to him by the Advocates of Helios and Stygios, and arrives at a decision based upon those arguments. However, the High Justice can preside over the Balance only if there *is* a Balance. If one side in the battle achieves such overwhelming power as to eradicate the other, then the function of the High Justice is made redundant. There is nothing it can do. That is the danger we now face."

"Spirit, why have you brought me to this strange place simply to speak of hopelessness?" Scrooge moaned.

"I am not speaking of hopelessness, Ebenezer Scrooge. Dire though the situation may be, all is not yet lost. There is one authority even higher than the High Justice, and it is to this authority that we of Helios are appealing."

"Who is this supreme authority?"

"You."

Scrooge stared at the spirit's pale, lovely face, dumbfounded. "This is a very poor jest, my dear."

Carillon shook her head. "It is no jest. You and the entirety of Humankind are the ultimate power. It is your belief and the belief of every man, woman and child that empowers and sustains the sides of Light and Darkness. It is from Humankind that the armies of Helios and Stygios are drawn, and it is their desires that are presented and argued before the High Justice by the Advocates of the Light and the Darkness. When Humankind no longer desires a yuletide celebration filled with joy and hope, when it wishes to dim its festive lights, it sends a powerful message that it is willing to be conquered by the Darkness forever."

In that moment Ebenezer Scrooge understood. There was indeed a desperate battle between the sides of Light and Darkness, of hope and despair, but it was not being waged on some otherworldly battlefield; instead it was taking place in every city, every town, every village and settlement on earth. He had witnessed the conflict every day on the streets of London; he had experienced it in his own life; but had never recognized it for what it was. Now Scrooge was aware that he had served as a foot soldier for both sides of the battle, without understanding the power that resided within him, resided within everyone. If the balance was to be forever shattered and the Darkness awarded the ultimate victory, then the High Justice was indeed powerless to prevent it; he was merely carrying out the decision of Humankind.

The words Carillon had uttered in the bedchamber of the Ghost of Christmas Present echoed in Scrooge's ears and served to chill him to the marrow: *He is dying simply because he is no longer wanted.*

The murderer of Christmas was Man himself.

"Dear heavens, what a fool I have been!" Scrooge cried. "What a blind, blithering fool!"

"Why do you chide yourself?" asked the spirit.

"When I realize how close I came to giving up, how close I came to drowning in an ocean of self-pity, what else could I do? How much has my own dark despair contributed to the poisoning of that noble figure in the other room? How much?"

"Despair is ambrosia to Lord Tenebra."

"Oh, I imagine it is, but he has consumed the last of mine, blast him!"

Carillon smiled, and her illumination seemed to increase in brightness. "You seem energized, Ebenezer Scrooge."

"The truth has made me so, and I have a message for your High Justice. There is just as much daylight left in the world as there is black night! I will tell you something else, spirit. If this blackguard Tenebra cannot even manage to convince a broken old sinner like me that it is time to give up, then he has no more power than a bedbug!"

Carillon laughed, and the airy, musical sound was tonic to Scrooge.

"Take away joy and replace it with despair, will he?" Scrooge shouted. "Turn humanity into a sullen goat herd and drive a stake of holly through the heart of Christmas, will they? Dim the lights of the season forever, will they? Hah! If this High Justice of yours needs proof that Humankind wants Christmas, then he shall have it! He shall have it if I have to undertake the journey to whatever domain he calls home, look him straight in the eye and deliver the message myself!"

The spirit laughed musically and clapped her hands. "I am very happy to hear you speak so, Ebenezer Scrooge," she said, "for that is the exact mission you must undertake."

FOUR

Far away from the House of Yuletide was yet another house of spirits, albeit of a different sort. The men at the rough-hewn bar of the Staggerd Inn——so named after a young stag, an image of which adorned the public house's sign, but ironically so, given that after a boisterous evening, most patrons staggered out——were regular customers. The smoke-filled, ale-smelling, hearth-toasted room was alive with conversation and laughter from men happy to be inside and warm on such a frigid night. When the door suddenly opened, sending a gust of vicious, icy wind through the pub, the men responded with a lively, off-key rendition of:

> *Shivery-shaky, oh, oh, oh,*
> *Criminy-crikey, ain't it cold!*
> *Woo-woo-woo oo-oo*
> *Pity the man what couldn't get warm!*

Closing the door as quickly as he could, the new customer turned to face the men.

"We've been waitin' for you, Davy!" cried Alvy Dock, a large, muscular man blessed with a bushy head of hair that had yet to see its first white thread. Alvy stepped aside and made space at the bar for the newcomer, while another man ceremoniously set a chair in the gap. Davy Slye quickly scuttled to the chair and climbed up on top, which was the only way he was able to see over the top of the bar, being as he was barely over three feet tall…in boots.

"A fine night to be blessed by the spirits," he declared, as a pint jar of frothing draught was set before him. He picked it up with a grimy black hand and raised it to his lips.

Anyone unfamiliar with the scene might have wondered why the proprietor of the public house would allow a child to come in and drink with the rest of the men from the village. But despite his tiny stature and bulrush leanness, Davy Slye was no child; he was a man who had grown as much as he ever would. Whereas some might have bemoaned this fate, having to spend their lives looking at the world from a child's eye view, the perpetually cheerful Davy considered it a blessing as it automatically provided him with a trade.

Davy Slye was known and regarded by all as the best chimney sweep in the county, if not the entire kingdom, and his profession explained the fact that at any given time he was so completely covered in soot that most had no idea what he looked like without it.

Davy drained the tankard and set it back down on the bar. "A hard day's work, it was, cleaning the flue of the Langham cottage," he said. "Better have another to wash down the ash."

"Better yet, ask Larrity to open a fresh cask o' the stuff and have a bath in it," said Alvy Dock, and everyone, including Davy, raised a chorus of raucous laughter.

As the owner and publican of The Staggerd Inn, Gabriel Larrity pumped a fresh pint into the glass and set in front of the little man. "Davy will come clean when he's ready," Larrity said. "I just hope I'm still around to see it."

No one at the bar would have placed a hard-earned shilling down in a wager that Larrity would be leaving his post any time soon, since he had been behind the tap house pumps as far back as anyone could remember. Many of

40

them could remember their fathers taking a stroll to chat with Larrity, and some rumored even their grandfathers had tasted their first ale from the hand of the burly, balding publican. Some in the village rumored that Larrity had been at his post since the reign of Henry the Eighth, and had, in fact, introduced Bluff King Hal to the pleasures of ale and fine wine. While that was hard for many to believe, it was also impossible to disprove.

"Will you be having another one, sir?" Larrity asked the stranger who had come into their midst a round of drink ago, drawing the glances of everyone else in the pub who were not used to seeing strangers——particularly one so well-dressed.

"Indeed, sir," the man said. "One more of the same, if you will."

Taking the gentleman's fine crystal mug (no common jar for such a one as he), Larrity refilled it with his most expensive bitter and set the foaming pint down in front of him. "It's always a pleasure to serve a new face," he said.

"The pleasure is mine, my good man. But I am remiss in allowing myself to be considered a stranger for so long. My name is Crimp, sir," he said, offering his hand, which the publican took. "Jasper Crimp."

"A visitor to our village, are you?" Larrity asked.

"I am. My business takes me to many towns and villages, and I have learned that there is no better way to discover the character and heartbeat of a community than to pay a visit to its inn or public house, so here I am." Then turning to address the crowd around him, Crimp added: "And gentlemen, as a gesture of goodwill to all herein, and in hopes of atoning for the royal freezing I gave all of you upon my entering, I would consider it an honor to provide the next round of drinks."

As Jasper Crimp dropped a half-sovereign on the bar a cheer went up among the men, and anyone who might have been harboring some secret reservation or suspicion against the well-dressed stranger immediately drowned it. For his part, Crimp endured cheerfully a series of poundings on the back, clappings on each shoulder, vigorous pumpings of his hand, and a tuneless toast to a Jolly Good Fellow.

Jasper Crimp pulled a long cigar from an inner pocket and placed it between his teeth and, taking his glass, stepped away from the bar and moved to the fireplace, looking for a stick with which to light his smoke. Finding none suitable, Crimp pulled a lucifer from his waistcoat pocket and struck it on the stone hearth, savoring the fleeting smell of brimstone as its tip burst into flame. Then he stood back and watched the men laughing, drinking and toasting.

Through the smoky haze of the pub Crimp could see that the patrons were hoisting an object up onto the bar, and at first he took it to be a filled black poke. To his wonder, it turned out to be a little man the color of coal. It required no great deduction to conclude that, given his size and sootiness, the little fellow earned his living as a sweep. At first Crimp thought he was being forced up there against his will, as a prank of some sort, but soon came to understand that the bar was the little man's speaking platform. "'Ush up, 'ush up," a voice cried, "Davy's gonna say somethin'"

Davy; Crimp made a mental note of the name.

Everyone quieted down——which in itself is quite a feat in a public house——as Davy's strong trumpet voice carried through the room.

"'Tis not often that a stranger enters this hallowed domain," he began, pronouncing the word *hallowed* as *hollered*, "nor is it common in my experience that one displays such a fine and generous spirit as we have seen here today." A dozen voices muttered in agreement. "Therefore I hope that all o' you will join me in an official toast to the father o' this round o' drink, Mr. Jasper Crimp!" The glasses, many of which were already empty, rose in unison. "To Mr. Jasper Crimp," Davy continued,

42

"friend to 'is fellow man. May he live a long and healthy life, and may he be in Heaven an hour afore the Devil knows he's dead!"

This was followed by another round of hearty cheers, and caught up in the spirit of the occasion, Larrity declared: "Aye and the next round of drinks is on the house!" The shouts and hurrahs immediately gave way to stunned silence.

"On behalf o' my ears, might I hear that again?" Davy asked.

"I said, you diminutive beer-sop, that the next round is on me."

Rolling his eyes and clutching his chest, Davy Slye shouted: "Ben's buyin'...my heart can't take the shock!" Stiff as a board, he fell off the countertop and into the arms of two laughing mates, who lowered him gently to the floor. "The little bloke's gone!" cried Alvy Dock. "The shock was too much for his ticker!" The rest of the men, Crimp included, and Larrity himself, laughed heartily at Davy's antics.

The publican pumped a new glass and handed it to Alvy. "Here, throw that in the little devil's face," he said, "and see if it revives him."

"'Ah, he looks perfectly happy where he is," Alvy replied, with a wink. "No need to waste a perfectly good pint wakin' him. I'll just take care o' this myself."

A voice from the floor cried, "Wait! Wait! I'm feelin' better already!" and amidst the laughter, the little sweep sprung up to his feet and reached for the glass.

"Thought that'd rekindle the spark o' life within you," Alvy said, winking again at Larrity, who roared in approval. Then with the well-practiced indignation of an opposing barrister, the publican shouted: "Now there's gratitude for you! This gentleman, Mr. Crimp, fine man that he is, comes in and buys a round for the likes o' you, and the roof timbers are nearly blown off by the hosannas!

43

But what does Larrity get in return for his generosity? Do I hear any singin', any tributes, any Jolly Good Fellowing? I do not." He *harrumphed* noisily, but continued filling the proffered glasses with free ales and stouts.

"'Tis the truth he speaks," Davy said, wiping the foam from his lips with the back of a sooty hand. "We have been remiss. So who has a song for our good friend and bennyfactor, Larrity?"

Only one volunteer came forward, an inebriate named Hawkins, who launched into a tuneless ditty concerning the lord of a manor and serving girl, but he was soon brought to silence on the grounds that the song was not quite fitting as a tribute.

"Come on, lads," Davy called, "this fellow has been single-handedly fightin' on our behalf against the Demon Thirst for as long as any of us can remember. And now you mean to tell me that not one man-jack o' you can come up with a song to repay him?"

A half-hearted repeat of "Shivery-shaky" welled up, but Davy similarly shouted that one down as not an appropriate tribute.

There was a prolonged silence as men looked self-consciously at each other, then from somewhere in the public house a youthful, vibrant, was heard singing, "God Rest You, Merry Gentleman, let nothing you dismay..."

Jasper Crimp snapped his attention toward the singer, who was young, not much older than a boy, as he continued: "For Jesus Christ our Savior was born upon this day..."

One by one the men took up the song until the tavern sang with one voice:

> *To save us all from Satan's power when we were*
> *gone astray;*
> *Oh, tidings of comfort and joy, comfort and joy,*
> *Oh, tidings of comfort and joy.*

44

Larrity had joined in, forgetting that the song was supposed to be sung in his honor. In fact the only person inside The Staggerd Inn who was not singing was Jasper Crimp, who stood by the crackling hearth, quietly smoking his cigar. When the singing had stopped, the tall, elegant man stepped to the middle of the room, savoring the opportunity that had been handed him. "An interesting choice of song, my friends," Crimp said.

"Tis nearly Christmas," Davy said, "and the gift o' free pints is as good an example o' holiday cheer as I can think of." A flurry of mumbled assents came from the men.

"Well, my friends, it was a fine song, finely sung, and don't let anyone tell you otherwise. And I hope what I am about to say will not offend any man here."

"Offend us, guv?" said Davy, "After the goodwill you've shown us tonight? 'Tis impossible."

"I will second that," Larrity said. "The Prince Consort himself, God bless him, could learn a few things about grace and generosity from you, sir, and that's a fact! And if he were to walk through that door at this very moment, I'd tell him so to his face." There was an underscore of agreement throughout the pub.

"Very well, then," Crimp said, with a wide smile, "no offense is presumed and I pray that none will be taken. I was merely going to ask all of you fine gents what was so special about Christmas?"

There was silence throughout the house. Then, as though he had not heard correctly, Davy asked: "What's so special 'bout *Christmas*?"

"Aye, my friend, what is so special about December the twenty-fifth? It is one day to be cheerful when there is really nothing to be cheerful about, the beginning of a celebration of joy where no joy exists."

"Christmas is special because...well, because it's Christmas," Alvy Dock offered.

"Ah, I see," Crimp responded, walking to the bar and setting his glass down. "Another if you would please, my good fellow. And if anyone would like to join me in another round, by all means, step up." The men did, but without the rambunctious cheer of before. Larrity filled the glasses in silence, and once each man had his fresh pint, Crimp toasted, "To your good health, my friends," then took a sip of the coppery liquid in his glass.

"I used t'like Christmas when I was a boy," said Felton Mersey, a sandy-haired man with large, work-scarred hands, whose tired eyes grew distant with memory.

"Aye," Crimp responded, "as did I, my friend, as did I. But we are no longer children, are we? Even you, lad," he said to the young man who had begun the song. "I daresay childish concerns seem long gone, do they not?"

All eyes in the pub were upon Jasper Crimp as he spoke in tones of great concern and empathy. "You are a man now," he said to the lad, who was known to the others simply as Young Geoffrey, "breaking your back from dawn to dusk for precious little wage, weighed down by the knowledge you can never stop, never rest, because you have a family to take care of, whether it be wife and children, or your fathers and mothers. Is that not the case?"

Many rough faces nodded silently and glumly.

Jasper Crimp took another sip of his ale and continued: "If it is little ones you have, then you return home each evening and there they are, waiting for you, looking at you, your sons and daughters, all of them too young to know the ways of the world. You look into their faces, gentlemen, the dear flesh of your flesh, and you see little creatures still living in a wonderful time, not yet burdened with the responsibilities of labor, a time when there is still magic in the world, when there is still Christmas. You look into those eyes, not yet ten years old, perhaps not even five, and you know how it is going to be for them in just a few years, maybe a very few years, and for the rest of their lives. You know, but you cannot tell them."

"No one had to tell me," Davy commented. "I was pushed down the flues to earn my keep afore I was seven year old."

"My response to that, friend Davy, is that you were raised by a wise man, whether he be father, uncle, guardian, or even beadle. You were taught early what the world is really like. I would never teach a child of mine that the world is a rosy place, playful and worry-free, only to have to snatch that illusion away forever when the time comes, and let the poor soul spend the rest of its life wondering why it cannot be like it once was. I would not teach any son or daughter of mine that one day a year magically wipes out all the cruelty and misery that man has to endure, as if it never existed."

"I take it then, sir," Larrity said, evenly, "that you yourself do not celebrate the holiday."

"You take it right, my friend," Crimp answered. "I do not celebrate any holiday connected with any faith, be it modern or ancient, accepted or pagan. I am a realist, sir, and as such I declare this special day called Christmas to be a sham and a fraud. It is nothing but a pernicious plot to weaken the minds of good men such as yourselves with false hopes and unattainable wishes. What benefit has Christmas been to any man here? Oh, certainly, you may have received a gift, some small trinket in honor of the holiday, but has that gift come freely? No, my friends, I suggest that it has not. Gifts are generally not given without the thought of something being returned."

"But you've given us a gift tonight, Mr. Crimp," Davy said hesitantly, "so what d'you hope to get in return from us?"

While Crimp was impressed by the mind that was housed in that sooty little body, at the same time recognized in him a potential opponent. People who could

47

think for themselves were to be considered suspect. But Crimp let none of his inner feelings show as he beamed his flashiest smile towards the little man. "You have found me out, friend Davy," he said. "There is indeed something I desire in return from you, and from the rest of you as well, and that is your friendship. I am a traveling man and like to establish friends everywhere I go. You see, I like to live by the creed 'Goodwill towards men,' every day of the year, not just the one day that has been designated for such goodwill by hypocrites who have no intention of charity towards anyone."

Crimp raised his glass to allow the beer inside to glow warmly in the firelight. "Look at the vessels in your hands, gentlemen," he said, "and ask yourself this: who was it that just filled that jar with fine ale in a spirit of goodwill and friendship? Was it Father Christmas? Was it Zarathustra? Or was it your servant, Jasper Crimp?" He bowed, just slightly.

For a long time no one said a word, the smoky atmosphere inside the pub having gone from that of a boisterous celebration to that of a funeral. Finally Felton Mersey spoke up: "I have t'admit, I always felt right let-down the day after the twenny-fifth."

"Of course you did, so have we all," Crimp said, "and the greater the merry-making the greater the disappointment to follow. A fine dinner, providing one can afford it, and a cheerful song has little enough power to erase an entire year of toil and pain. Gentlemen, I made the decision years ago to resist the myth of Christmas and embrace the world as it really is, no illusions, no deceptions, and have found myself a much happier man for it."

Finishing off his pint, Crimp stole a glance at his pocket watch then placed another half-crown down on the bar to cover the latest round of drinks. "My friends, it has been a rare evening, a fine evening, but I must be off." Wrapping a wool scarf the color of fresh hay around his neck, Crimp buttoned his greatcoat and secured his hat on his head. "Good evening, gents, I hope to see you again." Crimp then pulled the door open and held it open long enough to let the bitter cold rush in and sweep away any comfort, and then exited the pub.

He had not trudged ten yards through the bitter night's chill when he felt the dark presence fall into step with him. "I trust you are as pleased with this evening as you have been with others, my lord," Jasper Crimp said, looking straight ahead. "I doubt any of them will rush home with thoughts of Christmas goose and twelfth-night cakes."

No voice replied.

Crimp walked on in the presence of the shadow, a fact that did not comfort him. Lord Tenebra usually descended just long enough to give instructions or, like tonight, the occasional compliment, then lifted again and was gone. The shadow's lingering made him nervous. "Is something wrong, my lord?" Crimp asked.

Of course not. An unexpected setback, perhaps…but nothing that cannot be overcome. Still…

"Yes, m'lord?"

The other side has dared a tactic that I would not have believed possible. It shows how truly desperate they are. The last words blew through the silent, dark, cobbled streets of the village.

"Is it something I must attend to?"

When the time comes, I will attend to it myself.

The clop-clop-clop of a coach echoed past him and then Crimp saw a dray come into view, rounding a corner. As it neared, though, the horse whinnied and shied away from him, finally rearing up in fear and nearly tipping over the wagon behind. The driver cursed the frightened animal as he struggled for control, but the horse was too badly spooked to settle down. It bolted, hauling the out-of-control cart through the narrow street of the village, and ultimately out of Jasper Crimp's sight.

The beasts always know when we are about, Lord Tenebra said. *Unlike men, they know we are here. Unlike men, they know to fear us.* While Jasper Crimp never thought of himself as a born frightener of horses, he thought it best to agree with his Master. *We must be on our guard from now on…There can be no error…*

Then the presence was gone, leaving the black night considerably less black.

"Aye," Crimp said softly, shaking off his nervousness and feeling a great sense of satisfaction. No village was too small to approach and conquer in the course of his crusade. Tightening his scarf, he whistled as he walked down the cobbled street, his thoughts on tomorrow night's task and destination——his final.

It would be the eve of Christmas, representing both his biggest challenge and his greatest triumph, if he was successful.

If, Crimp admonished himself with a self-satisfied chuckle. There was no *if.*

Whatever was causing his Master concern, it did not extend to him. Crimp had never failed in his tasks. Never.

Nor would he when the objective was so closely in reach.

FIVE

The dim, cold stone chamber fell into silence; the only sounds Ebenezer Scrooge could hear were his own heartbeat and the wheezing, rattling moan of the Ghost of Christmas coming from the adjoining room.

"Carillon, I feel terrible, but you mistook my words just now. I was not speaking literally. How can I explain it? When I said I would go to the High Justice myself, it was a boast. When under the influence of excitement I have been known to say things that I later have cause to regret."

"Then all is lost. Any festival of light anywhere in the world will be dimmed forever."

"Surely there is someone else who could go; someone of greater youth and greater strength."

"In order to convince the High Justice, the testimony needs come from a man who has walked both sides of the conflict and who has already made a personal choice to disavow the Darkness in favor of the Light. It must know that such a choice is still possible for Humankind. You, therefore, must speak on behalf of your race."

I cannot believe that I am the only mortal who has made such a choice!"

"You are the only one who is accustomed to visitations with the spirit realm as well." The spirit's radiant face cast an imploring expression. "Please, Ebenezer Scrooge, there is no more time for rumination. There is but one day until Christmas. You must be on your way."

51

"Will you be there with me when I face the judge?" Scrooge asked.

"It is not my place to visit the high Tribunal," the spirit replied, "though others of the Light will be there with you. You will not be alone, Ebenezer Scrooge."

Scrooge tried to take comfort in that thought, as he prepared to take his leave, but a strong sense of apprehension was in him. "What if——" he began.

"Yes?"

"What if I am unsuccessful in carrying out this mission?"

"Do not think of such things."

"My dear, it is easy for you to say that, since you are not bound by the laws that govern mortals. You do not have a body that aches from exertion or gets weary from the sheer weight of years piled upon it. You are not made of corruptible flesh and bone. What certainty do I have that I will be successful?"

"There is no certainty, Ebenezer Scrooge. There is only faith and trust."

"How comforting. Very well, I will go. How am I to arrive at this High Justice's tribunal of yours?"

"Transport has been arranged, but first you will need to don these," the spirit said, gesturing toward a coat and hat rack that had suddenly appeared in the corner of the room. On it was Scrooge's greatcoat, its pockets stuffed with gloves and a scarf, and his tall beaver hat. "The journey will be cold indeed."

Scrooge put on the outer-garments and then turned to see Carillon standing in front of an enormous wooden door that a moment before had not been there. It opened of itself and the two walked out into the evening. Upon hearing the door close again behind them, Scrooge turned to look and saw...nothing. There was no door. There was no building. He was now standing on what appeared to be a country lane.

"I shall never get used to these otherworldly occurrences," he muttered, and at that moment the sounds of horse's hooves were heard, and two lanterns were seen far down the road, but rapidly approaching. When it neared, Scrooge could see it was a coach pulled by two white horses, and driven by a man clad in a heavy Ulster coat and a short top hat. The carriage stopped in front of them.

"You are here to transport me to the tribunal of the High Justice?" Scrooge asked the coachman.

"Yes sir," he replied, tipping his hat.

"But is the Great Hall not on high?"

"It is," said Carillon.

"But how can a common coach transport me to the heavens?"

"Well, sir," the coachman said, "the team is very *spirited*, you might say."

"Climb inside, Ebenezer Scrooge," the spirit bade him. "There is no time to lose."

"Very well," the old man said, opening the door of the coach and stepping in. When he closed the door and looked back through the window, the Carillon was gone. "Goodbye, my dear, wherever you are," he called. *I wish I could thank you*, he added mentally, *but only time will tell if you have indeed brought me any comfort.*

The coachman cracked a whip to spur the horses into action, and the carriage bolted forward and continued down the road. Slumping back into the leather seat, Scrooge wondered, certainly not for the first time this evening, whether this was nothing more than a bizarre dream from which he would wake up, shaken by safe and sound. He wanted to believe that, but was forced to admit to himself that he had never experienced the sensation of cold in a dream, or even a nightmare…certainly not the sort of cold he was now feeling.

He wished in vain that he could have brought Fanny with him, but she was very likely curled on, or under, his bed, safe and warm.

The coach bounced and shook with every pebble and rut in the road, as coaches are wont to do, but suddenly he felt it gaining in speed. It was no longer shaking or bouncing, either. Looking out the window, Scrooge saw the road which was cut through the countryside, illuminated by the moon, but he saw it from increasing distance. The coach was no longer *on* the road, but rather above it, and gaining altitude! At one point in his life Ebenezer Scrooge would have reacted with shock and alarm at such a vision, but no longer; he had seen too much of the other side of existence to question what was happening. He was in an airborne coach, and that was that. Soaring like a bird over fields, villages, and rivers, he felt a strange sense of contentment. If nothing else, he was being allowed to experience a miracle of sorts that would likely never be duplicated by another human being.

The journey was taking quite some time. A glance at his timepiece could have told him exactly how long, but it would hardly have mattered; choosing to go on this strange, nocturnal mission had been his last controllable decision; what happens from this moment forward, he sensed, was completely out of his hands. After a while he closed his eyes to rest, feeling that he might need it to conserve his strength for whatever was to come.

He had nearly been lulled into a light sleep when he felt the coach suddenly shake, as though it had been struck by an object. He opened his eyes and glanced through the window, wondering if the carriage had come too close to a tree branch. But it was still soaring through the night sky far, far above any woods.

When the turbulence struck a second time, Scrooge opened the window and leaned out to call to the driver. "Is anything wrong?" he inquired.

"It looks like we're in for some rough weather, sir," the coachman called back. "Best prepare yourself."

"Rough weather?" Scrooge echoed, peering up at the clear sky. The ground below had disappeared into the darkness, but there appeared to be no trace of a thunderhead anywhere around the carriage.

At once the cab dipped and bounced as though it had been struck by another vehicle, the force of which nearly deposited Ebenezer Scrooge on the floor.

"What is happening?" Scrooge cried.

"It's him, I'm afraid!" the cabman shouted back.

"Who?"

"The Lord of the Darkness! He means to prevent us!"

Unseen forces buffeted the cab back and forth and up and down, causing Scrooge to cry out, though his voice was nearly drowned out by the frightened whinny of the horse. Through the window Scrooge could see only darkness, as though the light of the moon had been extinguished like a gas lamp. One jolt against the carriage was so violent that Scrooge flew off of the seat and banged his head on the ceiling, then fell back down to the floorboards.

The coachman's voice called out, "I cannot hold the steeds!" and the entire cab turned over sideways. Ebenezer Scrooge tumbled onto the side of the cab and felt the door, now beneath him, come open. "Nooooo!" he shouted as the coldness wrapped itself around him. He tried desperately to grasp onto the seat, to anything, but he could not, and in another instant plummeted through the open door.

For the second time in this strange and terrible night, Ebenezer Scrooge felt himself tumble helplessly through the air, unable to discern where, if anywhere, was up and what was down, the cold stinging his face as he fell. In a matter of seconds he was absorbed by the vaporous cloud sea beneath him, and while it dampened and chilled him, it could not catch him or even slow him down.

As Scrooge continued his plummet to the earth, far below, the only sound he heard was a dark, ominous, satisfied laughter. Then his senses gave way to nothingness.

SIX

Tom Bray had always been big. He was probably born big, but his birth was something he could not remember. Ducking his head in order to enter his stone hut had become so commonplace to him that he never thought about it, but this time he forgot to duck and banged his head on the rough wood lintel. That was because there were so many other things on his mind that he was forced to struggle mightily to keep them all in order, meaning a few got lost. There was only so much room in Tom Bray's head at any given time, and at this moment, it was filled to capacity.

Much of what was in Tom's mind were things that were misunderstood by everybody else: horses, for instance. They were considered dumb beasts by everyone else, but Tom knew better. A stable groom since he had been a child, he had literally grown up around horses. He not only knew everything about taking care of them, he was able to communicate with them; not in words, but in understandings. He could look at a white stallion or a roan and know what they were thinking, what they were feeling, and he sensed that they could do the same with him. Tom regarded his horses as equals and did not presume that he was their better in any way. That could be why the animals accepted him so freely, unlike people, who often challenged his understanding beyond its limits, leaving him puzzled.

For instance, Tom Bray could not understand why so many men and women thought they were superior to other men and women. Neither did he understand why they wished to show that through clothing and decoration. A group of squirrels did not drape fripperies around themselves in order to look down at plainer members of their kind. Another unanswerable question was why the men who went to the building known as the "pub," where Tom occasionally took a solitary meal, drink so much when only one glass was enough to quench the thirst? Animals drink only what they need.

Most puzzling of all to Tom was why so many men and women pretended that true things had to be changed, while untrue ones were proper. A hare would not bind itself in some trap-like garment in order to look smaller and then pretend to ignore the discomfort, the way the mistress of the manor did. Neither would a fox that knowingly stole a hen from a coop lie about it later to its fellow foxes.

On this morning, though, a different puzzle occupied Tom Bray's overstuffed brain, one that he pondered as poked the logs of the fire he had built to warm his hut. He could not understand why no one had come out to see the man who had fallen out of the sky and landed on the ground nearby. Tom had, after all, told the groundskeeper, Mr. Stern, about the man's appearance earlier that morning. Yet no one had come out from the house to see the man, who was now lying on Tom's simple straw bed, for himself.

Could it be possible the people in the house thought Tom was lying when he reported discovering the man? That notion, which entered Tom's mind like a sudden fever, caused his brow to knit and his features to darken. Why would they not believe Tom? With his own eyes he had seen the man fall out of the sky the night before, surrounded by a strange white light that stayed with him as he fell, dimming only after he'd landed on a heap of fallen tree branches and needles, which looked as though they had been spread there deliberately to catch him. With his own hands Tom had examined the man searching for any signs of injury in the same manner he would a fox, a deer, or any animal in trouble, finding nothing more than a lump on the back of the man's head, which was probably the result of hitting a tree limb. As he carried the unconscious figure inside his hut, the old man's eyelids never once fluttered or blinked, and his thin face bore no indication of fear or pain, but rather an expression of peace. That struck Tom Bray as particularly odd since a fall from such a height must have been scarier than falling down a well.

At no time did Tom stop to wonder from whence the man had fallen. That, he figured, was the man's business.

As Tom sat in his hut pondering all this, a low moan escaped from the lips of the elderly man, and the groom rushed to his side. The man opened his winter-colored eyes and examined Tom Bray's face, his face betraying a sense of puzzlement. Then he slowly lifted his head and surveyed the inside of the crude hut. "Where am I?" the man asked weakly.

"Tom Bray's home," Tom answered.

Struggling to raise his head, Scrooge asked, "And who are you?"

Tom's brow knit at the silliness of the question. "Tom Bray," he said.

"That makes sense," Scrooge muttered. "How did I get here?"

"You fell from the sky."

"I did *what*?" Bolting upright, Scrooge felt a sudden sharp pain at the back of his head and touched it, finding a sizeable knot.

"Your head is hurt," Tom Bray said.

"Indeed it is," Scrooge said, as he continued to examine the strange, rustic quarters. The floor was earthen and the only furnishings, aside from the straw bed, were a handcrafted table, a chair, and a wooden trunk. A fire pit oven was built into one wall of the hut, serving as both the hearth and the stove, and some simple cooking utensils hung next to it. There was only one door, a heavy, oaken one, and one small shuttered window.

But basic as it was, the place seemed perfectly suited to the young man who was now studying him. Scrooge judged him to be roughly twenty years of age, perhaps a bit more, perhaps even a bit less. It was hard to tell. What was not in question was Tom Bray's size, both in height and breadth. The young man's large, probing eyes and wondering expression gave his face a childlike mask of innocence, but at the same time there was a seriousness about him that was so intense as to be almost comical, like the face of a child pretending to be an adult. A thatch of dark hair framed the young man's broad face.

Tom Bray pulled a dented metal cup from a hook on the wall, then dipped it into a water bucket and offered it to Scrooge, who took a sip of the cool, fresh water that was quite pure and sweet tasting.

"This is not from a well," Scrooge said. "Where do you get it?"

"From the sky," Tom Bray said. "When snow melts."

"I see. Well, Mr. Bray, I do not recall the circumstances that brought me to your house, but as long as I am here I might as well accept your hospitality in kind." Scrooge extended his hand. "I am...I am...oh, dear!"

Tom took Scrooge's hand with some hesitation, as if he were inexperienced with the custom, and said, "You are not a deer."

Perhaps the man was hurt worse than Tom realized.

"Great heavens, I cannot remember my name! I do not know who I am!" Dropping the young man's hand, Scrooge wandered through the circular hut as though in a daze before facing Tom again. "Have you ever seen me before, Mr. Bray?"

Tom Bray shook his head.

"This is terrible! What am I to do?" Scrooge cried. "Wait, where am I? Let's start there."

"Tom Bray's home."

"Yes, yes, but what city? Are we in London or nearby?"

"By the village."

"*What* village?"

Tom shook his head, uncomprehending. Here was here, and the village was the village, and that was all. There had never been any reason for him to put a name either to Here or to the Village. Then a thought struck him and Tom added, "Near the hall."

"The hall? You mean a manor house? Good, but which hall? Please, Mr. Bray."

"Old...castle."

"An old castle? We are by an old castle? That is helpful. Is this Warwick, then? Arundel?"

"No," Tom said, "Old...castle Hall."

"Oldcastle Hall," Scrooge repeated, but that name meant as little to him as did his own identity at present. He thought hard, trying to awaken any memory about his life prior to finding himself inside the tiny hut, but all his mind's eye registered was a swirling grey mist. "Can you tell me anything else?"

Tom Bray's eyes seemed to smolder from concentration, then suddenly a flame ignited behind them, and he said: "The river!"

"Ah, we are by a river, are we?" Scrooge said. "Very good. Which river?"

Just as suddenly as the light appeared, it was snuffed out again, and Tom Bray merely shook his head. It was the River. That was all.

"This is getting us nowhere," Scrooge sighed, suddenly aware of the stuffiness within the cramped hut. "I must get some air, perhaps it will help to clear my head."

"Come back," Tom Bray implored.

61

Scrooge intuited that Tom Bray most likely did not get very many, if any, visitors. "I will indeed come back, Mr. Bray."

"Not Mr. Bray...Tom."

"Very well, Tom. I simply need to go outside and think for a bit, or at least try to. Do you understand?"

The groom nodded and Scrooge went out, pushing the heavy door closed behind him. He was in a large clearing in a wooded area that was completely undistinguishable from any other such forest clearing. He could not see any geographical features, such as hills that might offer a clue as to where he was. With no memory of how he came to be in this place, Scrooge could do nothing but hope his cognizance returned, or that someone familiar with him would find him.

There was nothing else he could do.

Meanwhile, inside the stone hut, Tom Bray was arranging and straightening what few pieces of furniture he had to make it more presentable to his visitor. He smoothed over a gouge in the earthen floor and neatly straightened his heavy wool blanket, in case the man who fell from the heavens wanted to lie down again. This he managed to do by the time he heard footsteps nearing his door, and even before the caller had a chance to knock, Tom swung the door open to welcome his first ever guest. But the man who now stood before him was not the one who had fallen from the sky.

"May I come in, Tom?" asked a very thin, stork-like man in servant's livery, who was shivering violently in the cold. Without a word Tom stepped back, permitting entry to the man. "Thank you," said Osmund, who was the butler at Oldcastle Hall. He proceeded straight to the oven and said, "Please close the door again, Tom, or I shall catch my death of cold!"

Before doing so, though, the groom poked his head out and looked around, coming back in only when certain that no one else was out there waiting to enter.

"I have come straight from the hall, Tom," Osmund began. "The Squire has been informed of this man of yours, the one you found this morning."

"The man who fell from the sky," Tom Bray said, nodding.

"Quite so, though I fear the Squire was somewhat skeptical regarding the veracity of this report. Therefore, I thought I would nip in myself, hoping perhaps to meet this unique gentleman and inquire first-hand as to his person and his, er, unusual means of arrival." Tom Bray's expression clearly indicated that the servant's words had left him lost. Upon seeing this Osmund tried again: "Tom, where is the man who fell from the sky?"

The brawny man shrugged.

"But you said he was here in your house, did you not?"

"Yes."

"And yet when I look about your house, Tom, I do not see a visitor. Why is that?"

"Because he is not here," said Tom.

Osmund shook his head as he pulled out the chair and seated himself. He had always been patient with the stable groom, certainly far more patient than his employers, particularly Lady Oldcastle, who could never understand why on earth Tom Bray was not turned out into the forest with the rest of the wild creatures he loved so much. But the fellow was hardworking and conscientious, and Osmund had never seen horses get better care than they did through the strong and gentle hands of Tom Bray. The personal fondness Osmund had developed for the young man was the reason he found himself so disappointed with the prospect that Tom was deliberately lying. "If I may be blunt, Tom," he said, "the Squire claimed that your story was absurd. He believes there was no man at all. I ventured

63

out here in the freezing cold in the hopes of being able to argue against his harsh judgment. Yet I find no such man. What am I to tell the Squire now?"

"He will come back," Tom said.

"How do you know?"

"He said so."

"Then you absolutely maintain that the man was here earlier."

"Here. In the bed."

Osmund regarded the groom for a second and then moved to inspect the straw bed and blanket. *Does this provide any comfort and warmth at all in the bitter winter?* he suddenly wondered as he ran a hand over the surface of it. Concern for Tom Bray aside, the bed provided no evidence to support Tom's story. "There are no traces that a man has lain here recently, I fear."

"I made it neat," Tom explained. Then he realized that his words were not being believed, and the feeling hurt him. Eyeing the servant with an intense, searching look, he pointed to the bed and said emphatically: "He was here! Here!"

"All right, Tom, all right. It is nothing over which to upset yourself. If you say the man was here, then the man was here, for I have never known you to tell a falsehood of any kind. You, more than any other man I have ever met, live in the realm of truthfulness."

Tom Bray nodded. He did not fully understand all of the thin man's words, but his manner and tone of voice was placating.

"I must return to the hall now," Osmund told him, "but I would like you to do something for me. When the man returns from whatever journey he has embarked upon, please entreat him to come up to the house so that everyone there may greet him as well."

"Have him go to the house?"

"Yes. Will you do that?"

Tom nodded in agreement.

"Thank you, Tom. I am depending upon you. Now I must be off." Osmund opened the door and faced the frigid wind with obvious distaste.

Had the servant taken the time to inspect the wooded area around Tom Bray's house, rather than dashing across the snow-dotted grounds as fast as his spindly legs would carry him back to the hall, he might actually have encountered the man he sought, who was now weaving his way through the trees, trying to piece together any fragments, however small, from within his consciousness that might reveal his prior life.

He halted at the sight of a fat squirrel that darted in front of him. As he watched, the squirrel likewise stopped, sat up on its haunches and glared back at him. This forced a laugh from Scrooge, who said to the creature: "If you have any knowledge of who I am, I would appreciate hearing it."

Hear it he did: a long, loud chattery scolding that seemed to accuse Scrooge of every crime on the books, which made him laugh all the louder, which in turn made his head ache. There was nothing that the squirrel, or any other part of the woods around him, could reveal about his predicament.

Following his own footprints pressed into the snowy ground, Scrooge started back towards the home of Tom Bray. On the way he passed a bush with sharp leaves and clusters of red berries. It was a holly shrub, of course, but holly was not uncommon in England, meaning he could be anywhere on the island. Then a word flashed through his mind, one that was spurred by the sight of the holly...a single word that resounded so forcefully within him that it seemed to have been spoken aloud. With growing excitement Scrooge ran towards the house of Tom Bray, dwelling on the message that some unknown part of his mind had encoded in one meaningful word: *Christmas*.

SEVEN

"Tom!" Ebenezer Scrooge shouted as he burst through the doorway of the hut, his face flushed and his eyes wide with excitement. "Tom, what day is it?"

Tom Bray looked back at him, puzzled. To him, all days were the same, as they were to horses and deer.

"Please, what is the day?" Scrooge asked again. "Is it the twentieth, the twenty-first, the twenty-fifth? At least tell me what month it is. December? January?"

The groom silently shook his head.

"How can I make myself understood?" Scrooge muttered. Taking Tom gently by the shoulders, Scrooge looked into this open face and asked, "Is the New Year upon us yet?" but received only a confused look in response. "What about Christmas, then. Do you know of Christmas?"

A smile broke out on the young man's face. "I like Christmas."

"Excellent! Now this is very important. Has Christmas happened yet?"

Tom furrowed his brow in thought, then said: "No."

Scrooge sighed, and lowered himself into the chair. "That is good. At least I think it is." Tom was still looking at him with puzzlement. "You see, Tom, for some reason I have reason to believe that Christmas is at the heart of my identity. *Why* I am convinced of it I cannot begin to explain, but the word *Christmas* is the first real memory I have had since arriving here, the first real clue to who I

66

am." It was now stuffy and warm in the hut and Scrooge took off his scarf and coat, draping them across the straw bed. "Do you know how many days remain until Christmas?" he asked.

Without a word, Tom Bray went to his wooden chest and opened it, and then looked around the hut as though he expected someone unseen to object. Satisfied that he was alone, except for his guest, he was alone, Tom pulled out two interconnected rings made of rough paper. The object was immediately familiar to Scrooge, although he could not recall the circumstances under which he had last seen one. The rings were the remnants of a paper chain, the kind that children make and use to count off the days that remain until a special date, tearing off one link each day. Tom held up the links for Scrooge to inspect, and then tore one off.

One ring left meant that tomorrow was Christmas. Scrooge was left with one day in which to solve the mystery of his being.

Tom put the remaining link back in the trunk and closed the lid, his face a picture of misery.

"Why do you look so sorrowful?" Scrooge asked. "You said that you liked Christmas."

Tom nodded.

"Then why do you hide your holiday decorations?"

"Not good," Tom said quietly.

"Not good? Why, I think it was a fine chain."

"Christmas is not good," the young man said morosely.

"Christmas is not good? Who told you that?"

Gesturing in a direction that meant nothing to Scrooge, and keeping his eyes downcast, Tom said, "Squire."

"Squire? Who is he?"

"Squire Oldcastle. Oldcastle Hall."

"Ah, I see. As the master of the house he is in a position to set the rules, and he has said that Christmas is not to be celebrated, is that right?"

The groom nodded, then muttered: "He said Christmas is foolish and Tom is a fool."

"Do you believe him, Tom? In your heart do you really believe him?" Even though he heard no sound, Scrooge saw the young man's lips form the word *no*.

"I could have guessed that was the case, because I have seen nothing about Tom Bray that suggests he is a fool. Christmas foolish indeed! I would say it is your master who is engaged in folly. Do you want to know something, Tom? I don't believe Squire Oldcastle either. You don't believe him and I don't believe him. Therefore the fellow is out-voted. It is two against one!"

"Two against one," Tom repeated, mulling it over, then suddenly a broad grin broke out on his face and he laughed, a pure youthful giggle of delight. "Two against one!" he laughed, and wrenched open the chest once more, pulling out his paper link and proudly brandishing it before him. Finding a twig on a woodpile branch, he fashioned a stand to display the holiday decoration and he set it on the table, still beaming.

"How does it feel to be in the majority, Tom?" Scrooge asked, and the young man did not answer, but nodded vigorously. Then in the next instant he became very still and appeared to be listening, though Scrooge could hear no sound whatsoever. "They are calling me," he said.

"I hear nothing."

Looking to the door, Tom Bray said, "The horses."

"The horses are calling you?"

"They need me," he said, taking a heavy sheepskin coat from the chest and donning it. He was nearly out of the door when he stopped suddenly and turned back to Scrooge, and said, "They want you at the house. The thin man said so. Come back after going?"

It was spoken as a question.

"I will, Tom. I will come back here when my business at the house is finished."

The brawny man nodded. "The thin man is not like others," he said. "He is kind." Then he grinned at his new guest and left to care for the horses.

"What a singular young fellow," Scrooge said, studying the newly-mounted paper link. Inquiring at the hall was the best course of action, it seemed, but there was something he wanted to do first. Bundling up again to brave the cold, Scrooge went out to find the holly bush he had passed earlier.

Now seeing the clearing through slightly familiar vision, Scrooge realized that the patches of snow that alternated with squares of brown earth, green grass, and grey stone formed a lovely winter's forest quilt. The day not only looked fresh it *smelled* of freshness, and he drank deeply of the crisp air as he walked. Coming upon the holly bush again, he carefully broke off several branches, careful that the barbed leaves did not prick his hands even through the gloves. Before long he had more than enough for his task. Selecting from the pile the fullest branches with the greenest leaves and most abundant berries, Scrooge carefully arranged them into a sheaf he could easily carry and started back towards the stone hut. Having gotten his raw materials, he now wondered if Tom Bray possessed any twine, wire or ribbons with which to tie the pile of branches into a wreath. Strips of paper would hardly do for this. Surely they must have such items at the hall, he thought, if he found that Tom's supplies were lacking. Scrooge set his bundle down in front of Tom's door and set out for the manor house.

But where was it?

After inspecting the clearing, Scrooge discovered a well-trodden path that led through another patch of woods, and decided to follow it. Before long an imposing edifice soon came into view through the trees, a mansion constructed of reddish stone with three severe-looking gables capping the front and cattails of smoke from the

69

house's many chimneys rising up lazily against the slate sky. A foreboding iron fence that had at its center a tall stone gateway surrounded the house and grounds. Slipping through the gate, Scrooge walked briskly up the drive.

Stepping up to the front door, Scrooge suddenly realized that he was hungry, in fact, *very* hungry. Heaven alone knew when he had eaten his last meal. Aside from the sip of water Tom had given him, he could not remember taking anything in. As he rapped firmly with the lion's-head knocker, Scrooge hoped he might be able to talk the master of the house out of a joint of meat and a cup of hot tea as a length of ribbon or string.

A moment later the door was answered by a man dressed as a servant, whom Scrooge assumed to be the thin man about whom Tom had spoken. The adjective *thin*, however, was an understatement; the fellow could have hidden completely behind a lamppost.

"Yes?" the servant said, a look of confusion crossing his face, as though he was so confounded by the appearance of an unexpected visitor that he did not quite know what to make of it.

"How do you do, sir?" Scrooge began. "I was wondering if I might have a word with the master of the house."

The servant regarded Scrooge intently. "And who shall I say is calling upon the Squire?"

The question was inevitable, but Scrooge had been hoping against hope that it might not be asked, at least not before he had gotten inside the hall. "That, my dear fellow, is difficult to say, and unfortunately, a question I cannot answer."

"You cannot tell me who you are?"

"No, at the moment I cannot, because at this moment I do not know."

"Yet it is yourself who calls?"

"Yes. Believe me, I wish I knew who I was."

"I am terribly sorry, sir, but I fear that I cannot interrupt the Squire on behalf of a person who, no matter how refined his deportment may be, does not know who he is." Then the servant's face displayed dawning realization. Leaning in to Scrooge, he asked in hushed tones: "Are you, by any chance, the man whom Tom Bray found this morning?"

"I am."

In the next second, the servant grabbed hold of Scrooge's scarf and pulled him inside, quickly pushing the door shut behind him. "I *knew* Tom's word could be trusted!"

"I am afraid I do not understand."

The servant's professional composure instantly reappeared and he straightened up then bowed stiffly. "Do forgive me, sir, and welcome to Oldcastle Hall," he said. "I am Osmund, and am in the immediate employ of Squire Oldcastle. It is a pleasure to actually meet you, sir. I shall take you to the squire directly."

Scrooge did not understand why the man appeared to be struggling so mightily to stifle laughter at the thought of his meeting the master of the house. But before he could contemplate it further, his stomach issued a rumbling noise that practically echoed through the house.

"Did you say something sir?" Osmund asked.

"No, but I'm afraid my stomach did. I have not eaten anything since…well, I do not know since when."

"We shall have to remedy that, then. What do people from the sky eat?"

"People from…oh, yes." Scrooge recalled Tom Bray's claim that he had fallen from the heavens. Hoping not to jeopardize the prospect of a good meal, he decided to play along. "Well, I cannot speak for every human meteor, but I am rather fond of bacon, beef, ham, potatoes, eggs, puddings, bread, tea…" His stomach complained again, cutting off the list.

71

"Extraordinary," Osmund declared. "Please come this way, sir."

Scrooge followed the servant through the massive house, first into a sitting room in which no one sat, which was lined with books which no one was reading; then into the dining hall, its long mahogany table vacant, but with the aromas of an earlier meal remaining to torture Scrooge's stomach even further; down a hallway and through a music room, in which no one played; and finally down a staircase and into the large kitchen, in which a woman was cooking. Two young scullery maids were hard at work on a mountain of dirty dishes, but it was obvious that the true boss of the kitchen was the tallish, sturdy woman who supervised them between tuneless snatches of song, all the while carefully inspecting a pile of leeks and selecting the best ones, tossing those into a gleaming copper kettle.

"Mrs. Kenley, we have an unexpected guest in the manor," Osmund announced. "Please see to his needs and requests. His name is...is Mr. Plummet." The prim face of the servant curled slightly in appreciation of his own joke.

A sigh fell from the aproned Mrs. Kenley as she considered her new charge. "As if there weren't enough mouths to feed around here," she grumbled to Osmund.

"Forgive me if my appearance here is untimely," Scrooge said. "I have not yet had the pleasure of meeting the Squire or his lady."

"Pleasure ain't the word what comes to mind with those two."

"No, no, Mrs. Kenley," Osmund said. "We must be charitable. Our guest here says he cannot remember when he last partook of a meal."

The entire demeanor of the cook changed then, her face becoming a mask of motherly concern. "Don't know when you last et?" she said. "Why, you poor dear! That's a statement as makes my heart pump three times as fast and ache for the effort! Don't know when you last et? Why, you

72

just set your bones down right here and I'll have a feast up for you presently. Gracious! Don't know when he last et? Lucy, Molly, put down the plates and come here and help me set a meal for this poor man." Eager to put a halt to their workaday activities, even for only a few moments, the girls dried off their reddened hands and rushed to Mrs. Kenley. "Never let it be said that Rebecca Kenley ever let a soul get away from her table in a state of hunger!" the cook declared. "Not that I has to worry about *that* happening around here, mind you!"

After taking Scrooge's greatcoat and hat from him, Osmund bowed and then repaired to his other duties. For her part, the cook was as good as her word. After a brief but dexterous flurry of pans, pots and other utensils, wielded by Mrs. Kenley and her assistants Lucy and Molly, Scrooge had before him a steaming banquet of eggs, pork, bread and potatoes, and a pot of fragrant tea, which he initially set upon more as an animal than a civilized man. Then remembering his manners, and his pledge not to be a disgrace, he began to slow down and savor the food. When his breakfast was finished the dishes were cleared and placed on the stack as quickly as they had appeared on the table, and the two quiet maids returned to their daily drudgery.

As Scrooge was helping himself to another cup of tea from the ornate silver pot, Mrs. Kenley asked him: "What is it that brings you to this humble home?" Scrooge thought he detected a tone of sarcasm coloring the word *humble*.

"Well, madam——"

"Mrs. Kenley, iffen you please. Or just Cook, iffen you like better."

"Very well, Mrs. Kenley, I suppose you could say I am lost."

"Oooh, ain't that a shame," she said, having moved her attention from leeks to tomatoes, gripping one firmly and tossing it into her other hand with the skill of a professional juggler. "Wandering the earth lost and hungry. Tch, tch, tch. Next thing, you'll be telling me that you was rescued and brought in from the cold by Master Bray!"

Scrooge came very close to blurting out, *That is exactly how I find myself here*! but thought the better of it. Such a statement would raise questions that he knew he could not answer. After a moment's silence, he said, "I have met Tom Bray. He seems like a fine lad, though not much of a conversationalist."

"Tom Bray's got a heart as big as the earth itself. He's a strange 'un, though, Tom is. He's not like you and me. He's a creature of nature. Iffen there was a wild, mad horse tearing around, the likes of which you or I wouldn't dare approach without fear of getting trampled, Tom Bray'd just walk up to it easy as you like, stand there and pat it on the nose, and while you was watching, the two of 'em would get on just like they was having a nice little chit-chat, man-to-horse. And iffen Tom was to turn around and walk away, that horse'd follow him home, step for step, like a puppy dog."

"You have seen such things?"

"I have," Mrs. Kenley averred, drawing a chair up to the table and seating herself across from Scrooge to continue her tale. "One time there was this poor little vixen who got her leg in a poacher's trap right here on the property. The thing just cried and cried something terrible, sounding just like a baby. Mervyn, the Squire's regular coachman, found her, and he wanted to relieve the poor little thing of her pains. He went and got the gun that he uses for hunting and pointed it down at the fox's head." The woman sat back in the chair and crossed her arms. "Do you know what happened then?"

Scrooge shook his head, eager to learn.

"All of a sudden, Mervyn feels this hand on his shoulder and he hears a voice next to him say, 'No.' He looks around and young Tom is standing there, but he ain't even looking at Mervyn. He's looking right past him at the injured vixen. And the fox, she sees Tom, too. Like that she closes her mouth and stops crying, just looks back at him like he was family. And Tom walks right up to her as gentle as you please and opens up the steel trap with his fingers——he's a strong 'un, Tom is——and carefully takes out the fox's hurt foot. Then scoops her up and carries her home in his arms like a baby, and her glad to go! The very next day Mervyn is out on the grounds, and what do you suppose he sees?"

"I have no idea," Scrooge said, though in truth, he did.

"He sees Tom Bray resting in the shade under a tree, and that little fox is sitting in his lap! Her leg is in a splint that he's fashioned out of two sticks, and Tom is stroking her head like she was a calico cat."

Calico cat. An image flashed into Scrooge's head then, but scurried away just as quickly and mysteriously.

Mrs. Kenley rose from the table and turned her attention back to the basket of tomatoes, from which she selected one and began inspecting it. "That's why I spoke of your having been brought in from the cold by Tom Bray," she said, "because he takes care of poor creatures what need help."

"How does he know to do these things?" Scrooge asked.

"How does the sea know to be wet?" Mrs. Kenley answered. "Like I said, he's a creature of nature, Tom is."

"Has he been here long?"

"His entire life. He was a foundling, left at the door of the manor. Nobody knew who Tom's folks were, but Sir Edward, the present Squire's father, made him his ward. Even as a boy Tom had that magical way with animals. He started taking care of the horses from the time he was eight or nine years old and wasn't that a bitter pill for the old groom to swallow? But it was what Sir Edward wanted. When the squire passed away Tom stayed on. For a while he stayed here in the house, but that seemed to make Tom uncomfortable. Living in a room with a soft bed and plush furnishings was too much civilization for the boy, iffen you ask me. Finally he took up in that old smokehouse, and that's where he's stayed for nigh onto ten years now, content as an oyster."

While Scrooge had not considered the possibility that oysters were the very models of contentment, he accepted her judgment. Osmund chose that moment to return to the kitchen, his face betraying a bizarre amusement. "I have spoken to the master about you, sir," he said to Scrooge.

"And what did he say?"

The effort of trying not to laugh out loud caused the servants lips to perform acrobatics. Finally he said, "I fear that the Squire did not take the news particularly well. He maintains his insistence that you do not exist."

"Oh dear."

"He was most emphatic about it."

"Would it help if I presented myself to him?"

"And defy *Himself*?" Mrs. Kenley cried. "Ooh, Osmund, wouldn't *that* be a spectacle! Hoo-hoo!"

"It would be, would it not?" Osmund echoed, covering his mouth with his hand as he chuckled audibly. Once he had recovered he said, "Come, with me, Mr. Plummet. I shall introduce you presently."

As the servant led Ebenezer Scrooge up from the kitchen and back through the chambers and corridors of Oldcastle Hall, Scrooge was struck by its manor's lack of life. There were plenty of items to fill up the stately rooms and cover the richly-paneled walls; fine paintings and tapestries, the best furnishings and rugs, highly-polished silver candelabrums in every room illuminating the vastness; but none of it quite took away the feeling of emptiness in the hall, as though the building had only deigned to hold its occupants and their possessions rather than accept them.

Coming to an impressive polished oak door of a study, the servant stopped, and was about to turn the knob when a terrible cry came from the other side, sounding like a mad beast under attack.

"What in heaven's name was that?" Scrooge asked.

"The effects of snuff, sir," the servant said. "Do you partake?"

"I do not."

"Neither do I. What's more, neither does the Squire, at least not willingly. However, it has been the family industry for generations, with the Squire the latest of the Oldcastle line to command of one of the largest snuff-producing factories in the Empire, located here on the bank of the river Pindle. Thus is he duty-bound to examine the quality of the product on a regular basis. The result, alas, is the commotion you just heard." Motioning Scrooge to the door, Osmund cracked it open widely enough to peer into the room beyond.

Standing behind a table littered with several small containers stood Mortimer Oldcastle, squire of the manor and heir to the Oldcastle estate. He was short and round, and possessed a face that was as pale and doughy as a dumpling. With obvious reluctance, the Squire took a pinch of powder from one of the small ornate boxes that were lined up on the table in front of him, and whisked it up his nostril. Immediately his round face became so flushed and red that it appeared to be on the verge of exploding. The Squire drew in a series of breaths, each bigger than the last, none of which were released, until he had puffed up like a great fat pigeon, and was flapping his arms and hopping about as though attempting to take flight. That was when the explosion occurred: a sneeze that came with such force that it nearly toppled the man off his feet and produced the fearful sound Scrooge had heard through the door. Slumping against the table once the fit had passed, the Squire attempted to steady himself. Behind him a hidden door in the wall flew open and a woman passed through it. She was roughly the same size and shape as the Squire, though unlike his blanched, pasty face, hers was a palette of colors: carmine lips, rosy cheeks, and mauve around the tops of the eyes. She also wore a large, reddish wig, which slid slightly as she marched up to the Squire.

"Lady Oldscastle," Osmund whispered, somewhat redundantly, since Scrooge had already suspected as much.

"Would you cease that infernal racket?" Lady Oldcastle demanded of her husband. "I can hear it on the other side of the house!"

"I wish I could, my sweet," the Squire replied. "This batch seems worse than the last."

"I don't know why on earth you cannot employ a servant to test the stuff."

"You know that doing so would be breaking with a long-standing Oldcastle tradition, established by the Squire's great-grandfather. It is quite out of the question."

"What I know is that living in the bell tower of Notre Dame would be quieter."

"I shall endeavor to keep the noise down, my dear."

"Honestly, I don't see why on earth I must put up with this, week after week, month after month…"

From Scrooge's vantage point, he thought he saw Squire Oldcastle mouth the words, *year after year* along with her.

Lady Oldcastle turned around and disappeared through the door in the wall, slamming it behind her. Osmund similarly shut the study door.

"Even though I have no personal experience with or knowledge of snuff or its qualities," Ebenezer Scrooge said, "I can only conclude that the product must be inferior."

"All I can tell you, sir, is that if you were to ask certain men who labor in the Squire's factory whether or not they deliberately seed the test samples with the finest ground pepper, you would like as not get a conclusive answer."

"Good heavens."

On the other side of the door, another explosion was heard, though this one appeared to be muffled.

"Perhaps I should come back some other time," Scrooge said.

"No, sir, no time like the present." The servant rapped on the door and waited for the response.

"Yes, who is it?" the Squire's voice called.

"Osmund, sir. May I come in?"

"Be quick about it."

"Stay here," the servant told Scrooge. "I shall introduce you." Then he opened the door, and strode inside the study.

Still leaning against the table but now quite red-faced, the Squire looked up at him. "Well, you infernal heron," he said, "what utter nonsense are you promoting this time? Is a man from the moon joining us for brunch? A singing giraffe canvassing donations for the village fete perhaps?"

"Actually, sir, there is a gentleman who wishes to see you."

"What kind of gentleman?" the Squire asked suspiciously.

"A prosperous gentleman, I would say."

Was he prosperous, Ebenezer Scrooge wondered? The servant must have been commenting on his mode of dress which did indeed appear to belong to a man of means.

"Ah, I see," Squire Oldcastle said. "A prosperous gentleman has come to call upon the master of the house. An honor for both of us, I shouldn't wonder." The Squire flicked the remaining tobacco dust from his fingers, primped and smoothed his crimson vest, the buttons of which were dangerously strained. "It is always a pleasure to meet another member of the gentry. Such a traveler in this area is indeed a rarity, but when one such prosperous soul passes through, we must accommodate him. Don't just stand there, show the fellow in!"

Osmund turned and went back into the hall to usher Ebenezer Scrooge into the room.

Approaching Scrooge and dipping in a courtly bow before him, the Squire said, "How do you do, sir?"

"Your servant, sir," Scrooge replied, likewise bowing.

"It is very good of you to come."

"Thank you."

"I am Mortimer Oldcastle, esquire."

"I am...happy to make your acquaintance," Scrooge said.

"Do you care for a pinch, my good fellow?"

"Uh, no thank you."

"I do not believe I caught your name, my good man."

"This is Mr. Plummet," Osmund replied, by way of introduction.

"Ah...of the Nottingham Plummets?"

"I cannot say so," Scrooge replied.

"No matter. Why are you still here, Osmund? I am certain Mr. Plummet does not require the presence of a domestic to talk for him. He may speak on his own."

"Actually, Squire Oldcastle, that might not be the case," Scrooge said.

"I do not understand."

"Well, you see, my earliest memory is of awakening in the home of a young man named Tom Bray this morning."

"Tom Bray...this morning?"

"Sir, allow me to present to you the man who fell from the sky," Osmund said with obvious relish. "The one whose very existence you denied stands before you."

At once the face of Squire Oldcastle quivered, and he tore his gaze away from Ebenezer Scrooge as though Scrooge represented the most terrible sight on earth. Then spinning around so quickly that he nearly lost his balance, the Squire ran back to the table and repositioned himself behind it, as though preparing for an attack.

"What do you take me for, you blackguard?" the Squire demanded, keeping his eyes trained on Osmund only. "How many times have I told you that there is *no such man!*"

"I most humbly beg your pardon, sir," Osmund replied, "but my senses, at least two of them, tell me that the man I speak of is standing right here."

"Silence! Either you have taken complete leave of your senses or you have decided for some reason to carry out this ridiculous charade in order to hound and bedevil me! But whatever the reason rattling in that peculiar head of yours, I will have none of it, do you hear me? None of it!"

Clearing his throat, Scrooge joined the conversation: "I truly beg your pardon as well, Squire, but if I might be permitted to try and explain my predicament——" But the mere sound of Scrooge's voice had a profound effect on the Squire, who reacted as if he had been struck by a hard blow. Staggering back from the safety of the table, holding his arms out to steady himself, he asked weakly: "Did you hear something?"

"Just now?"

"Yes, you accursed skeleton, just now!"

"I believe your guest spoke," Osmund replied.

"No, no, no, no, no, no..." the master of the house chanted, closing his eyes and clapping his hands over his ears. "I have no guest, there is no man, he cannot speak, and one more word concerning this matter shall ensure your dismissal! Gods! Why must I be so tortured by my inferiors? It is a plot to drive me insane, I shouldn't wonder! Go, get out of my sight! Go and have your visions elsewhere!"

With a deep, sweeping bow, the servant backed out of the room, and then winked at Scrooge before disappearing down the hall. The Squire, meanwhile, ran to the door as fast as his stumpy legs would carry him, and slammed the door shut. "Man indeed!" he muttered as he returned to the table, mopping the sweat that had sprung up on his brow with the back of his hand, and taking no notice whatsoever of Ebenezer Scrooge.

Scrooge was completely baffled. He did not know his own name (and did not intend to adopt the one the servant had created for him), he did not know how he had come to be involved with the mad souls in this strangely lifeless house, and now he was trapped in a room with a man who was denying his very existence!

Having regained control, Squire Oldcastle attempted to act as though nothing at all had distracted him from his punishing task. He flipped open the next snuff box in the line and with an expression of grave trepidation took a pinch and sniffed it up, pulling a large white handkerchief from his ruffled sleeve in readiness of the inevitable. Within seconds his face was a bloated, crimson mask and he began hopping and flapping his way into another cataclysmic discharge. Waving his handkerchief limply in front of him like a flag of surrender, he staggered weakly to a chair and flopped down, exhausted.

"May I ask a question?" Scrooge ventured meekly. "Do you really not see or hear me, or is it simply that you deny me?"

"I deny you," the Squire answered, blowing his nose. Then with a look of growing horror, he cried: "I deny you utterly! I cannot see you, I cannot hear you! Why cannot you be reasonable and go and haunt someone who believes in you!"

"It is not my intent to haunt you," Scrooge said.

"Then tell me what it is you want of me, you malignant spirit?"

Spirit...

Why did *that* word resonate so suddenly and completely within Ebenezer Scrooge? There was something in the word that should have meaning for him, but what was it? Could it have any connection with the memory of

Christmas? Oh, how this half-memory frustrated him! Darting in and out of his mind, dancing around the edges of it like a shadow not wishing to be seen in full.

"First *Christmas*, now *spirit*," Scrooge muttered aloud. "Those words mean something, but why does my soul refuse to speak to me?"

"Because you are not really there," the Squire said. "What's more, do not speak to me of Christmas."

Scrooge recalled his conversation with Tom Bray. "I have been told that you do not celebrate it."

"Told by whom, Puss in Boots?"

"By Tom Bray."

"Bray again," the Squire groaned. "A simpleton who cherishes the holiday. Christmas is nothing but great expense and great trouble. Celebrating it would entail closing the plant for the day, letting the workers off for their personal revels and wagering that they will return in a timely fashion on the morrow."

Wager...Scrooge thought.

"And for what?" the Squire went on. "Because someone has decided that one day a year should be set aside to make merry! This Merry Christmas business is a curse wrapped in bows and disguised as a treat; it is a sham, a hoax, a...a...what is the word?"

"Humbug?" Scrooge offered.

"Precisely! I see you are a phantom of the world."

Humbug; another word that resonated with Scrooge, though he had no idea why.

Gathering his courage, the Squire drew himself to his full height (which was not considerable) and began to wonder why this pensive vision had ever frightened him. "I have quite finished speaking with you, sir," he declared, going to the door and opening it. "I expect to not see you again, and if by chance I do see you, I shan't acknowledge it! Now be gone."

Scrooge made his way out of the room, still caught up in the words that swirled around his brain: *Christmas*; *Spirit*; *Wager; Humbug*; vaguely remembered pieces of a puzzle that, when completed, would present a picture of himself. As the words coursed and collided in his mind, he remembered that he had come to the hall in the first place to ask for a bit of string or ribbon with which to make a wreath.

Unable to find Osmund, Scrooge retreated back to the kitchen where Mrs. Kenley was still bustling about her domain. Her face brightened at the sight of him, and drawing upon her good cheer, Scrooge asked if she had some ribbon and string with which he could forge a wreath for Tom Bray from the holly branches he had snapped. Within a few minutes, she procured from somewhere some lengths of red and yellow ribbon and a small ball of twine. Armed with this raw material for merry-making, Scrooge thanked her profusely and headed for the front hall, where he found his greatcoat and hat hanging on a rack by the door. Donning them, he set out trudge back to the hut of Tom Bray.

When he found no sign of Tom inside or out of the hut, Scrooge assumed that he was still attending to his chores and went to work fashioning a wreath with the holly branches, carefully tying them together with the ribbon and crafting them into a ring, whose shape he secured with the string. The final result might not have merited attention at an arts marketplace, but it was respectable enough, and brought a much needed spot of brightness to the humble home.

When Tom Bray finally returned, after the sun had set, the effect the wreath had on him was remarkable. A child-like smile graced the young man's face, which remained even as Tom labored to build a crackling fire in the oven, which warmed the hut and bathed it in a soft yellow light. Tom started to hang a heavy kettle over the fire, but then stopped. Still smiling, the young man turned to Scrooge and announced: "We will go out!"

"Will we?"

Tom nodded and hefted the kettle back to its storage place. "The pub," he said, and Scrooge figured that it meant going into the village. Bundling up against the cold yet again, Scrooge said, "Lead the way, Tom."

Both remained in good spirits as they tramped down the dark wooded road that led to the village; Tom because Christmas had been given back to him by his new friend and Scrooge because he was able to reward the young man's kindness with happiness.

All Ebenezer Scrooge needed now was his memory and life back.

EIGHT

A dark chill had descended upon the public house called The Twelve Bells that night, but it had nothing to do with the weather outside.

Instead of bursting with the sounds of boisterous life, it was as quiet and lifeless as a corpse. Old Ben——whose surname was unknown to anyone except, presumably, his wife——had operated the pumps for as long as any man in the village could remember. This night he drew as many pints as usual, but did so out of duty instead of with his customary good cheer. In response, his customers emptied their glasses mutely. There was no joking, no laughing, and no singing of songs. It was so quiet that one could actually hear the ticking of the ancient clock behind the bar, which Old Ben claimed had kept perfect time without being wound once in thirty years.

In the midst of this unnatural calm, Jasper Crimp savored the miasma of misery that permeated the room, which he had spent the last hour creating. "Another round, gents?" he asked casually, flicking the ash from his pungent cigar into the hearth.

"No," came the barely audible mutter from the men, who continued to stare into their mugs, or at their feet, or at the wall——anyplace except at one another. So focused were they on their inner blackness that no one noticed when the door of the pub opened to let in two more customers, two men who carried in the chilly scent of night on their clothes. In time the men looked up from their gloom, nudged and whispered to each other, and pointed at the new customers. Before too long, Tom Bray and Ebenezer Scrooge found themselves the center of attention.

"I'll be stretched," declared Robby Quill, who like most of the men in the pub labored at the Oldcastle Snuff factor, "Silent Tom has brought a friend with him."

"Good evening to all," Scrooge said cheerfully, but his good wishes clattered against the stony sullenness of the room.

"Evening, sir," Old Ben said with a nod. "Friend o'yours, Tom?"

"Yes, my friend," the groom answered, and for most in the establishment, it was the first time they had ever heard Tom Bray speak. Some reacted as though their favorite dog had suddenly started a conversation.

"Then ye be welcome, friend of Tom's, sir. The boys call me Old Ben. What be your name?"

"My good man," Scrooge said, wearily, "I could fabricate a story to cover my ignorance, but I simply no longer have the energy to do so. The truth is I have no idea what my name is." That declaration at least caused some stirring in the crowd of men.

"A man who don't know his own name?" the publican said, scratching the back of his thick neck as if that was where his brain was stored. "Let me see, we've had nearly every other specimen o' mankind pass through this humble house over the years, but a man who don't know his own name? I can't recall ever welcoming within these walls one of that ilk. It's a first! Ye are welcome here, sir." Wiping his foamy hand on his soiled apron, Old Ben held it out to Scrooge.

Scrooge took the man's hand.

"What will ye be having, my no-named friend?"

For the first time, Scrooge stopped to consider that he might not be carrying enough money to buy food or drink; perhaps he was not carrying any money at all. Quickly surveying his pockets, Scrooge came up with a small cloth purse filled with shillings, and for some reason he was able to determine how many he held simply by their weight.

How is it I am able to do that? he wondered, absently, but let the thought go.

Satisfied that he had the wherewithal to purchase a meal, he ordered up the fare of the day, a savory game stew and two mugs of hot cider for him and Tom, who seemed puzzled by his generosity, but did not complain. The two then made their way to a small rickety table in the corner, near the fireplace, not far away from where Jasper Crimp stood.

Crimp had been keeping a watchful eye on them since they entered. Tossing the end of his cigar into the fire, where it sizzled like a fuse, Crimp sauntered over to the table at which Scrooge and Tom were seated.

"I don't believe I've met you gentlemen," Crimp said.

Looking up, Scrooge studied the tall man's face. "I am a stranger here," he said.

"A visitor, as am I. The name is Crimp, friend, Jasper Crimp." Scrooge shook the man's hand, which Crimp then offered to Tom. "Good evening to you as well, young sir." Tom studied the proffered hand, even appeared to sniff at it like a dog, but refused to shake it. The young man's face showed an odd, dark expression of distaste, as though he had suddenly and unexpectedly found himself in the presence of a bitter enemy.

"My friend is rather bashful," Scrooge explained, yet even he was puzzled by Tom's reaction to the tall stranger.

"I understand," Crimp said, withdrawing his hand, with no visible hard feelings. "Though I do not share that affliction."

"Would you care to join us?" Scrooge asked.

"A most gracious offer, thank you," Crimp said, grinning broadly as he pulled a chair from a nearby table and seated himself next to Scrooge and Tom, who was

88

intently staring into his stew bowl and ignoring the tall man.

For his part, Jasper Crimp equally ignored Tom, who seemed to him duller of wit than a turkey. Instead he concentrated on Ebenezer Scrooge. "I always enjoy meeting new people in each town or village I visit," Crimp said. "Much of my time is spent traveling, you see. Business demands it."

"What business are you in?"

"Mankind is my business, you might say."

A powerful bolt of memory shot through Scrooge's mind. Where had he heard that phrase before? Why did it seem to him so important? Someone he knew, knew well, a long time ago...someone who had left him and had then returned unexpectedly...but who...what...?

"Are you all right, my friend?" Crimp asked.

With a shake of his head, Scrooge forced his mind to return to the present. "What? Oh, yes, I am fine."

"You appeared to leave us for a moment, sir."

"I became lost in thought, but the thought darted away again. I am sorry, Mr. Crimp, what was it you were saying?"

"Nothing so portentous that it bears repeating. You still look to be a bit shaken, however. Are you certain you are not feeling poorly?"

"I have no complaints that cannot be explained by carrying the weight of sixty years on my shoulders." *Sixty*! Scrooge thought. *I know that I am sixty*!

Crimp continued to scrutinize him. "I would offer to buy you a drink, sir," he said, "but it appears that you are not a drinking man."

"Not much of a drinking man, I confess," Scrooge replied, glancing at the remaining hot cider in his mug. "As to whether I once was at any time in my life, I cannot say, since that information is lost to me. However, a special occasion is coming upon us very soon, one that should be celebrated with as much merriment as possible. Therefore, I would be delighted to raise a special toast, even without the benefit of hard spirits."

Jasper Crimp smiled slyly. "By all means, sir."

Rising from his chair, Ebenezer Scrooge held up his mug and called out to one and all: "Gentlemen, I should like to make a toast to Christmas!" Each man in the pub became as a statue, glaring at him with expressions of incrimination. Even with all the doors and windows fastened tight a new chill had infiltrated the inside of the pub.

"My heavens," Scrooge said, sinking back into his seat, "I said *Christmas*, not *murder*. I mentioned the most joyous time of the year and receive tombstone looks in return! Perhaps they did not understand me."

"Oh, they understood you perfectly, my friend," Jasper Crimp said, silkily. "I daresay there is nothing wrong with either their understanding or your speaking. It is just that the lads do not hold Christmas in as high of regard as you do. In fact, I would lay a bet that you could sit here for a fortnight and not once hear the name of Father Christmas invoked by any of the honest souls present."

"Why is it that everyone in this town seems to think that the celebration of Christmas is harmful?"

"For my money you've hit the nail on the head. There is indeed harm in the celebration of Christmas, great harm."

Tom Bray, meanwhile, had become so drawn into himself that even Ebenezer Scrooge momentarily forgot he was sitting next to him.

Jasper Crimp continued: "I can tell by the look on your face, my friend, that you do not believe me when I speak of the harmfulness of Christmas. Let me ask you, then, what happens the day after Christmas? After the goose is eaten, the presents unwrapped, and the merry made?"

"Things revert back to normality," Scrooge answered.

"Precisely, and if one is living in a palace, then perhaps normality is quite pleasant. But for those not named Victoria or Albert the world continues just as it was, not having stopped in its bleak reality for a single second, not even slowing down, and most of all, not even caring. Things that had to be done on December the twenty-fifth still have to be done on December the twenty-sixth, the only difference being that they are one day late. Misery that existed on the twenty-fifth is still there the next day; it has not gone away, it has merely been ignored. The harm of Christmas, my friend, the true, palpable harm, is that Christmas is the enemy of reality, the giver of false hopes. The world would be so much better without it."

Ebenezer Scrooge said nothing.

"I see you have become convinced of the wisdom of my words, my friend," Jasper Crimp said quietly.

Scrooge turned and looked into the man's dark eyes, so intently that Crimp flinched slightly. "Not in the slightest," he said. Then rising again, holding his mug aloft again, Scrooge declared: "I say to anyone who will listen that harsh reality is the hand that all men are dealt, and they make of it what they will. But hope and joy and celebration are the things that men make for themselves. We have no sway over reality. Celebration, however, is entirely up to us, and we can make it or no. So once more I ask, who will join me in a toast to the celebration of Christmas?"

At first no man in the public house moved; each one remained frozen in place, like so many figures in a wax museum. Then, slowly, Tom Bray rose to stand beside his friend, tightly clutching his mug of cider. He glared at Crimp, his eyes burning defiantly into the other man's, reducing Crimp's ever-present smug grin to a wary grimace. "Two against one," Tom said, so softly that only Scrooge could hear him.

"Ah, what the hell," a voice called out, and Old Ben raised a glass behind the bar. "I'll drink to Christmas with ye!"

"I'll raise a jar to Christmas, too," cried Robby Quill, and one by one, the men gathered around, mugs and glasses raised high, to toast the holiday.

His face darkened with suppressed rage, Jasper Crimp glared at Scrooge. "Who are you?" he demanded.

Before Scrooge could make a reply of any kind, the pub door flew open and a booming voice cried out, "*God Himself!*" Jasper Crimp spilled his bitter down the front of his expensive waistcoat.

The door closed again as suddenly as it opened, cutting off the cold gust of wind, and all eyes turned on a newest visitor, who repeated in orotund tones, "God Himself would freeze on a night like this!" The speaker was a thickset man of middle age with a bushy mane of white hair. If the man had ever possessed a neck, the evidence of it was long gone, as his head rested directly atop his brick body like a rock set on a chimney. He was hatless (though his hair was thick enough to offer protection through all but the heaviest storms) and instead of a greatcoat he wore a wide, sweeping cape.

"Criminy, another newcomer!" Old Ben cried at the sight of the fellow. "The village must be playing host to a convention of strangers! Evening, sir," he called to the white-haired man. "What can I get for you?"

"For the nonce, nothing," the stranger thundered, "however, after the performance a libation or two would be most welcome."

"The performance of what if I might ask?"

"I am glad you did, my good fellow. I am Thaddeus Macaulay!" The white-haired man paused as if awaiting recognition and acknowledgement. When none came, he pressed on. "I have the honor of being the manager as well as the leading player of the Thaddeus Macaulay Theatrical

Company, widely renowned in the provinces of England, and other places as well. It is with great pleasure and pride that I announce that the Thaddeus Macaulay Theatrical Company will be performing this very night in this very community!" The oration was made with such power and theatrical flair that some of the men succumbed to the speaker's "clap-trap" and felt compelled to applaud, a response that Macaulay accepted with long-practiced graciousness.

So overwhelmingly had this new visitor commanded the attention of everyone inside the public house that nobody, not even Scrooge, noticed that Jasper Crimp was no longer among their number. Crimp had slipped out of The Twelve Bells shortly after Thaddeus Macaulay had taken its stage.

"If I might be so bold as to raise a question, sir," Robby Quill said, "your bein' here in our village and offerin' up a performance to boot is a trifle peculiar."

"This is the reaction that often greets me from the public at large," Thaddeus Macaulay replied. "Why, you may be asking yourselves, is the Thaddeus Macaulay Theatrical Company not instead performing on the stage of the Paris Opera House, or *Teatro alla Scala* in Milan, or before the Tsar of all the Russias? Why is it here in this humble, rustic little village? Because, gentle people, *this* is the life's blood of the English theatre! Let others parade their garish pageantry in the palaces of Europe. Let those more arrogant than I force their audiences to come to them, rather than reaching out to touch, to entertain, to inform the common men and women of the provinces. I, my friends, wish to be one thing only: a player for the people. And that is why I...am...here." He bowed to another smattering of applause, and a whistle or two.

Old Ben say, "That is admirable indeed, sir," Old Ben said, "but I think what Robby meant by it being peculiar is that this village has no theatre."

Straightening up suddenly, Macaulay boomed, "That problem, my good sir, has been remedied. A fine and generous patron of the arts who does business here has kindly allowed a parcel of property to be used for the exclusive purpose of the production of a dramatic event by the Thaddeus Macaulay Theatrical Company! And as an expression of gratitude for this wonderful little community, I should like to invite each of you to be my personal guests for the performance this very evening."

"Are we to understand, sir, that you are opening your doors at no charge?" the landlord asked.

"That is correct, sir, a performance by the celebrated Thaddeus Macaulay Theatrical Company at no personal cost to any man in this room! Consider it a seasonal gift, if you wish."

"And a most generous offer it is," Ebenezer Scrooge said, joining the throng around the actor-manager. "Not moments before you entered we were speaking of Christmas, the season of giving." His eyes darted around the room, searching for Jasper Crimp, who was nowhere to be found. "Perhaps some of our collective Christmas spirit has influenced you in this decision, eh?"

Making his way to Scrooge's table, the bombastic thespian said, "Actually, sir, I must confess to you that while Thaddeus Macaulay is only too glad to offer one of his signature productions *gratis* to an eager public as a gesture of good will and token of the season, there is in actuality another reason. It so happens that we have a new playwright among us, a reasonably talented lad to be sure, but uncertain of his own abilities, and untried before an audience. We are scheduled to open in Bath in a fortnight, and this poor lad has hardly slept one night in the past week, worrying about the reception his work will receive. If I do not put his play before the public so that he may gauge their reaction and make appropriate changes, I am fearful that our author might come down with such a case of nerves that he will explode! Positively *burst*!"

Even though many of Thaddeus Macaulay's words were far out of Tom Bray's reach, the young man was riveted to the strange, stentorian man whose bearing and manner was completely unlike any man he had ever seen before, and upon the man's last statement, he gasped. Knowing a captive audience when he saw one, Thaddeus Macaulay focused on Tom, transforming his eyebrows into the wings of a soaring gull, and added, "Like a sausage!"

Tom's eyes grew to white saucers.

"We would not want that to happen, would we, my large, working-class friend?" Macaulay asked Tom, who shook his head vigorously. "Then you must come and prevent the terrible occurrence." Turning to the general assembly once more, Thaddeus Macaulay exclaimed, "We shall be at the old Battersby warehouse on the bank of the river. Now I must leave you and get back to my merry little troupe. The curtain, such as it is, will rise promptly at eight o'clock." Marching to the door, which he threw open as though an assault on the night, Thaddeus Macaulay cried: "Once more into the breech, dear friends, once more!" and with a final flourish and swirl of the cape he was gone.

"I want to see the man explode!" Tom said eagerly, his face that of a small, excited boy who has just seen his dream of a Christmas present in a toy shop window.

"I believe that was merely an expression of speech, Tom," Scrooge said, chuckling, "but indeed, we shall go see the play."

"Play?"

"A drama, Tom. Actors playing roles in order to tell a story. Have you never experienced a play?"

The big man shook his head.

"Dear me. Well, I believe you will enjoy it, as long as you understand it is not real. It is merely show."

Examining the expression of puzzlement on Tom Bray's face, Scrooge realized that the young man had no conception of theatre. Perhaps it would be best not to attend whatever revels the bombastic actor/manager had planned. It was his choice.

Choice.

Dear God, there it was again! he thought; a word, a thought that carried the weight of an anchor yet held no more meaning than a cloud. Something in his forgotten past had involved a choice, perhaps a series of choices.

Given that context, the decision to attend or not attend a play in a makeshift theatre seemed singularly unimportant, yet it was not. He sensed it. Somehow it was not simply important, but vital.

Turning to his friend, Scrooge said, "Tom, I would like to see the play, but if you do not wish to, I understand. I will try to find my way back to your home on my own after the show."

Tom Bray shook his head. "There are two of us," he said. "Two against one. Two will see the play."

"We had better be on our way, then, while seats are still available," Scrooge said, with a smile.

NINE

Jasper Crimp walked the dark night alone, his face and hands buffeted by the bitter wind, the aroma of burning wood from every chimney of every house in the village cruelly taunting him with the promise of warmth inside...for others. Even colder than Crimp's flesh, however, was the icy chill he felt in his chest.

While not a man who succumbed to fear easily, he was frightened and apprehensive. Never before had he failed at his task, and tonight of all nights! But this was one small village among the dozens he had visited. Surely this one failure was not enough to make a difference when measured against all of his prior successes. Surely his Master would understand that.

Except for the cool pale moonbeams that bathed the village in an eerie blue, there was no light, and save for the hard tromping of his boots against the cobblestones, no sound. He did not hurry. There was little use in hurrying. What Jasper Crimp knew was tracking him was something that was impossible to outrun.

Shivering as he walked past the last of the cottages on the road to the next village, Crimp thought it was impossible to be any colder than he already was. But when the Darkness suddenly descended upon him like a black, shadowy shroud, he realized he was wrong.

"My lord," Crimp uttered, and in opening his mouth he let in air so cold as to freeze his teeth.

Why did you leave the public house so unceremoniously? demanded the voice that was carried on the frigid wind. *Why did you abandon your task and steal away like a thief in the night?*

"In the bracingly cold night, my lord."

Your comfort is of no concern to me. My appetite has not been sated; the sweet misery and despair that I crave have not been served up in adequate portions. What transpired this evening?

Swallowing hard, Crimp stopped walking. He did not look in any particular direction; the shadow was everywhere. "I thought it best to leave the pub, my lord," he said, his voice barely above a whisper. "Sometimes it is wiser to flee a battlefield than to continue to fight and cede further ground."

You retreated entirely...like a common coward. There was a dangerous quality to the airborne voice.

"My lord, I had little choice. The men of the village were distracted by a stentorian buffoon who stumbled in with the offer of theatrical entertainment, which temporarily deflected my efforts. It is a momentary setback that will pass, I assure you."

What buffoon? the shadow rasped.

"Macaulay, he said his name was. Thaddeus Macaulay."

Macaulay...I know of no such man. He will not present a challenge to us...as long as you carry out your duties successfully.

"You can count on that, my lord. Now that I know what he offers, I will be able to counter it."

Do so, my servant.

"Aye, my lord," Crimp, resuming his walk to the inn. "It will be an even simpler job if I can keep him separated from that old man who speaks of Christmas and his human ox companion who listens."

WHAT OLD MAN? the voice roared.

In an instant Jasper Crimp felt like it was being torn from his chest by an icy hand. "My lord..." he gasped frantically.

WHAT...OLD...MAN?

"I...don't know...my lord," Crimp said, struggling to breathe, fighting to remain conscious. "He...said he...could not...remember...his name."

DESCRIBE HIM!

"Please...my lord..." Crimp begged, and as the icy clench in his heart subsided, he fell to his knees. When he was able to speak again, he said, "He said he was sixty years of age, white-haired, sharp-featured, scrawny but possessing an aura of strength."

The sound of a nightmare thunderhead shook the ground upon which Jasper Crimp knelt, only Crimp knew it had nothing to do with the night's weather. Finally, the rumbling formed the words: *It cannot be he.*

"Your nemesis, my lord?" Crimp panted. "The old man from London of whom you have spoken?"

He was dealt with...I can no longer feel his consciousness...It cannot be he...Unless I have been tricked!

The very notion that the Master of Darkness could be outwitted provided Crimp with the most terrifying moment of the entire evening. "I do not understand you, my lord," he whimpered.

Any time I cannot sense the consciousness of a traveler it means they are dead. Yet...if a man has been robbed of his consciousness...while remaining alive...I have underestimated the cleverness of our enemies. So have you, Crimp.

"I beg, then, that I be forgiven for the same sin to which you have succumbed. Remember, my lord, it was I who informed you of the old man's existence. Otherwise you would have continued to think him dead. I acknowledge fully that I blundered in not recognizing him, but now that

99

my grievous error has been corrected, we still have a chance to vanquish him."

After what seemed to Crimp like an eternity of cold darkness, the sepulchral voice said: *Rise, my servant.*

"Thank you, my lord," Crimp said, pulling himself upright on shaking legs.

Mark me, Crimp, the time for errors has long passed. There can be no miscalculations, no misjudgments.

"I shall not err, my lord."

Who is the old fool's friend, this...human ox of whom you spoke?

"He is a villager named Tom, my lord, but the man is simple. He cannot pose a threat. If the Light is now recruiting village idiots as travelers, I would argue that we have already won."

His function may be unknown to him. He may have been chosen as the protector of the old man without understanding anything of his role. He is not so much a traveler, Crimp, as an unwitting knight errant. As long as the old traveler remains unaware, he cannot complete his mission. He cannot be allowed to regain his memory. There seems to be only one course of action, Crimp.

"And that is?"

Kill him.

Jasper Crimp's mouth fell open. He had never actually taken a life while in the service of the Darkness, and he never wished to. His power was that of persuasion, of argument, which he used to depress the happy moods of his fellow men. Wantonly taking the life of another, however, was as common an act as it was distasteful, and Crimp prided himself on being neither common nor tasteless. "My lord, if I may offer another possibility——"

There is no other possibility... the old fool must die at once, and it must be through you...I can influence humankind, I can destroy spirits...but the only creature that can murder a human is another human.

100

"My lord, you have other mortal travelers under your influence who would, perhaps, be better suited to the task."

Only you have encountered the man. None of my other servants could act with the required speed. There is only you, Crimp.

"My lord, I have never asked you for anything——"

Neither have you defied my orders before.

The words cut like a scalpel.

"I am not defying you, my lord, I am simply..." Jasper Crimp lowered his head. "Very well, I will of course obey you."

Yessss, the voice hissed, *you will, though mark me, the old traveler will not die easily. He should have died any number of times already. His heart is strong and his commitment to Helios is stronger still, despite all my efforts.*

"I will do what must be done, my lord," Crimp said.

I will not tolerate failure.

In the next instant, the shadow was gone, and Jasper Crimp sank back down onto his knees, completely spent. "I will not fail you," he said, but in his heart, Jasper Crimp, for the first time since coming into the service of Darkness, felt true fear. He personally cared little whether the Light was eradicated or the Balance remained intact, Jasper Crimp's primary goal was to remain alive, comfortable, and unburdened by terror. There seemed to be no other way to ensure that goal except to carry out his Master's orders.

He must kill the old man, and probably the man's simple bodyguard as well.

TEN

It did not take long for the battalion of men to make their way through the blistering cold from the Twelve Bells to the run-down warehouse. They took seats on whatever was available: benches, an odd chair or two, barrels and overturned crates. The building was dusty and smelled of tobacco, and was illuminated by a row of lanterns lined up on the floor as well as a few hanging down from the roof beams. The "stage," as defined by the lamps, was further masked on each side by cleverly arranged crates to accommodate the entrances and exits of the actors.

Spying what appeared to be a covered hay bale, Tom Bray rushed to it and sat on one end, waiting for Scrooge to catch up and take the other. While not the most comfortable of seats, they offered an excellent view of the stage area.

After all were seated, the granite-hewn figure of Thaddeus Macaulay stepped out from behind one of the false walls and received a generous helping of applause. Stuck to the thespian's face was a false beard of chestnut-brown, which clashed violently with his snowy hair, and draped over his blunt body was a long robe. On his head was a wreath. From his elevated vantage point, Ebenezer Scrooge suddenly tensed at the sight of the image. That robe, that wreath, that luxurious beard, all of it was important to him, yet he was unable to understand why.

"Thank you, my friends," Macaulay crowed, dining on the applause as though it were the world's most succulent goose. "Thank you, non-patrician patrons of the arts!" He stepped forward and raised his hands for the applause to cease, and once it had, he announced: "It is now the privilege and pleasure of the Thaddeus Macaulay Theatrical Company to present, in its first presentation on any stage a new work titled, *Cavorting with the Spirits of a Christmas Eve*, for which we beg your humble patience, pray, gently to hear, kindly to judge our play!" The last few words were delivered with such grandiose thunder and sweeping gestures that some of the audience in the would-be playhouse rose to their feet to applaud the orator. After a few moments of this great acclaim, Thaddeus Macaulay bowed formally and dashed behind the makeshift scenery.

As the title *Cavorting with the Spirits of a Christmas Eve* ran through Scrooge's head, a shadow memory licked at his brain like a flame, though not so close as to leave a mark. He turned his full attention to the playing area, onto which a sour looking man in a tall hat now strode. Heavily made up to simulate the ravages of age, the actor hobbled on to the accompaniment of artificial snow, which was being dropped by a young man precariously perched atop a wobbly, and badly concealed, ladder. Two other men, one tall and thin and the other short and plump, emerged from the other side of the stage, broadly pantomiming a conversation with each other. Upon seeing the hobbling man they approached him.

"Ah, Mr. Sludge!" cried the short, round man, while his tall friend said: "It is Mr. Sludge, is it not?"

"It is," the hobbling actor replied in a tight, pinched voice, which sounded every bit as crabbish as he looked.

"Mr. Ezekiel Sludge, of the firm of Sludge and Marrowbone?" queried the tall one.

"Yes, yes, yes, what of it?"

"Why, nothing of it, sir!" cried the other, sweeping his hand into the air for no apparent reason. "Nothing, except that we are taking up a collection to benefit the city's poor

103

and disadvantaged. Now then sir…now then sir…now then sir…"

A look of panic engulfed the man's face until a youthful voice from behind the crates whispered: "How much can we put you down for?"

That voice, Scrooge thought, *I have heard it before.*

"Ah, yes, thank you, my boy," the actor muttered, then loudly and authoritatively repeated: "How *much* can we *put* you *down* for?"

"The poor? The *poor?*" cried "Ezekiel Sludge," so clearly outraged that many in the audience gasped at the sheer force of it. "I will tell you about the poor! They are poor because they *choose* to be poor! Let them work for a living the way I have, the way Mr. Marrowbone did, rest his soul these seven long years. Show me a poor man and I will show you a lazy man. Speak to me not of the poor, gentlemen, the myth of the poor is a fraud, it is nonsense, it is humbug!"

A wave of grumbling passed through the audience, which was largely comprised of working poor men, after this speech, but Ebenezer Scrooge hardly noticed. His mind was racing so rapidly in all directions that it nearly crashed against itself.

"Ezekiel Sludge" finally succeeded in getting past the two bothersome men and crabbed his way off the stage. "Heavens!" cried the portly actor, stepping downstage to get out from under the shower of artificial snow. "If Mr. Ezekiel Sludge is not the meanest, hardest, stingiest miser in all of England, I shall be hanged!"

"I hope never to meet a more grasping one!" the tall actor added. Their point having been made, the two then strolled off the stage to a smattering of applause. Ebenezer Scrooge, however, remained still.

From the opposite side a man hastily pulled an old stuffed chair onto the playing area, and then announced to the audience, "The home of Ezekiel Sludge," before darting off again. Sludge followed the chair onto the stage, shaking the artificial snow from his hat and coat, picking at some that had become lodged in his exaggerated white eyebrows, which looked artificial enough without it. "The poor," he growled dramatically, "I wish I had a copper for every man, woman and child in the world who desires to live off of the bounty of others by hiding behind the label of poor! I would be rich indeed!" Then stepping towards the audience, taking them into his confidence, he added: "Actually, I *am* rich indeed!" He threw off his coat, placed a nightcap on his head and lowered himself into the chair. "The poor," he went on, obviously enjoying himself, "Humbug! And Christmas——there is the greatest humbug of all. The grand humbug of the world! Once every year honest souls such as myself are expected to sanction the avarice of the lazy, simply because it is Christmas. I will no longer tolerate it!"

Scrooge's body grew taut as he watched Ezekiel Sludge rise and make his way to the front of the playing area. "I tell you, it is humbug. Humbug!" Another murmur rippled through the crowd, but Ebenezer Scrooge paid no attention. With each repetition of the word *humbug* he had reacted as though struck.

Sludge went back to his chair, curled up in it and within seconds was "asleep" and snoring loudly. Then a low moaning came from somewhere behind him: "Slu-u-u-u-dge!"

Sludge groggily mumbled "Hm...? Wha...? Who's there?"

"Ezekiel Slu-u-u-u-dge!" the voice moaned again, and the actor sat upright.

"Show yourself!" Sludge demanded.

The owner of the moaning voice did show himself, and the display provoked gasps from the rapt audience. The small figure's huge black eyes stared out from a dead grey face, which was cursed with an impossibly long nose and cheeks that seemed sunken through to the other side. A fellow actor would have recognized it as a wonderfully effective and painstaking job of theatrical makeup; the audience, most of whom had never actually seen the presentation of a play before this night, merely shivered and shuddered at the ghastly sight. Tom Bray was among the latter category; he put his hands to his mouth and shrunk back in a gesture of fear.

Scrooge felt his breath catch in his throat as he watched the action, but for a different reason.

"Who...who are you?" Sludge gasped, cowering.

"I was your partner, Joseph Marrowbone!" the specter moaned.

"Joseph? You have traveled far to see me."

"I come from the other side, Sludge."

"Why have you come?"

"To warn you."

"Warn me? Warn me of what?"

"You have one last chance to change your miserly, cold-hearted ways, Sludge."

Scrooge's mouth fell open as the memories flashing in his mind began to slow down and come together.

"Joseph, I thank you for your troubles," Sludge said, "but I am an old man. I cannot be expected to change." He rose from the protection of the chair, becoming bolder in the face of the grotesque creature: "Besides, why would I want to?"

Drawing in a deep breath, the figure of Joseph Marrowbone let out a howl so unexpected, so horrifying, that the crowd gasped in unison. Tom Bray emitted a small cry of terror.

"Howl, howl, howl, howl! Oh, you are a man of stone!" the ghost shouted with great relish, as Sludge dived behind the chair, quivering violently. "I tell you that you must change, Ezekiel Sludge, or else end up as I, walking the earth eternally, denied the peace of mortal men who have crossed to the other side."

"What must I do?" "Sludge" whimpered.

"You will be visited by three spirits before dawn. You must welcome them and go with them. They will guide you along the pathway of redemption. And if you comply you will be spared my fate. You will discover that the true purpose of man is to help his brother man, and, most importantly, Sludge, you will learn to appreciate and revel in that most glorious Day of Days, *Christmas*!"

This last word was delivered as if to shake the rafters of the warehouse, but it was nearly drowned out both in force and enthusiasm by another cry, one that came from the audience. Even the actors on stage stood in stark confusion and watched as an old man seated in the back of the audience leapt to his feet atop the hay bale and began to jump up and down, crying: "Ebenezer Scrooge! Ebenezer Scrooge! Oh, my heavens, *my name is Ebenezer Scrooge*!"

ELEVEN

As for the rest of the people in the makeshift playhouse, if any one of them genuinely cared what the future held for miserable old Ezekiel Sludge, they were destined for disappointment. From the moment of Scrooge's outcry, the play fell irreparably to pieces.

Joyful exhaustion finally halted Ebenezer Scrooge's leaping dance atop the hay bale. His face flushed and beaming, he grabbed the hand of Tom Bray and pumped it vigorously, saying, "How do you do, Mr. Bray, I am Ebenezer Scrooge," as though they had only just met. Tom's growing distress at the bizarre actions of his friend was apparent in the sudden tension of his body and in the bafflement on his face, but Scrooge patted his arm reassuringly. "I am not mad, I assure you, Tom, merely overjoyed that I have remembered who I am and what it is I must do! I am Ebenezer Scrooge!"

"Eben...ezer Scrooge," Tom said thoughtfully, thinking it an odd name indeed. But if that was the name of his friend, then he would accept it. "Ebenezer Scrooge," he said again, in an effort to become accustomed to it.

One by one, the upstaged and now purposeless actors poked their heads out from behind crates and flats and wondered what all the commotion was about. From the center of the maelstrom a voice roared: "*Silence!*" Instantly mouths shut, limbs ceased moving, and all faces turned towards Thaddeus Macaulay, who now stood at the center of the playing area, spotlighted by the gaze of thirty pairs of eyes. He marched rigidly towards Ebenezer Scrooge, some of his company falling in line behind him, and fixed a withering glare upon the old man. "Do you know what you have done, sir?" he demanded in a doomsday voice. "Do you have any idea?"

"My dear Mr. Macaulay," Scrooge began, "I humbly beg your pardon and assure you that I do have a defense for my actions if you wish to hear it."

"*Hear*?" Macaulay roared. "*Hear*? I have already heard you, sir! How could I fail to have heard you? I daresay they heard you in the colonies of America! What else *was* there to hear while we poor players attempted to strut and fret our hour upon the stage, only to be heard no more… *because of you*?" The line of players behind Macaulay gave him a respectful ovation.

"My dear sir, words cannot express——"

"Words! Names! Amaimon sounds well; Lucifer, well; Barbason, well! Your words, my good man, have caused more damage than the Great Fire of London!" Even though Thaddeus Macaulay was not a particularly tall man, his carriage and bearing were such that he gave the impression of looking down upon the apologetic Scrooge. "What you have done this evening has not been accomplished in the history of theatre. There is one great principal of the stage, sir, and that is that the show must press on. If the actors are ill, the show presses on. If the theatre is flooded, the show presses on. If enemy soldiers from a hostile land march into the playhouse, sabers drawn and muskets pointed, the show presses on. But you, sir, have done what disease, disaster, and invasion have not managed to accomplish in three thousand years: *you have stopped the show*!" Raising his arms in a martyr-like pose, Macaulay then dropped his head until his chin rested on his chest. After a second, his hands dropped like birds in a shooting party. The company of actors standing behind him, after a moment of awed silence, responded with wild applause and cheers, and even

Tom Bray, eyes wide and filled with wonder, joined in, clapping loudly.

"Sir, please, if you are finished," Scrooge said.

"Finished!" Macaulay cried, suddenly springing back to life. "That is indeed the word! Thanks to you, I am finished, and so is the Thaddeus Macaulay Theatrical Company. Each and every one of us, finished! Ruined! Demised!"

"Permit me a moment of explanation, Mr. Macaulay," Scrooge entreated. "I will not bore you with the details, but up until this very night, practically this very moment, in fact, I was a man without a past, unaware even of my own name. Try to place yourself in my position, sir; your name unknown, your whereabouts unknown, your entire life gone like so much smoke. This was my state of being upon entering this building tonight." Though his voice was much quieter and less bombastic than Macaulay's, Ebenezer Scrooge nonetheless held the audience. "Then as I sat here watching your play, my self-awareness returned to me like a bolt of lightning streaking down from the heavens. I suddenly knew I was Ebenezer Scrooge of London. Certain aspects of your drama, by the most incredible coincidence, reminded me of my own life."

Macaulay regarded him like a visitor to the zoological park contemplating a vaguely human primate. But in the next instant visions of broadsheets danced in his head: *Ruined life regained through performance by the Thaddeus Macaulay Theatrical Company*! Or better yet: *Thaddeus Macaulay, noted thespic artiste, saves man's life*! Yes, that one was definitely better. Macaulay's entire demeanor changed and the roaring lion gave way to a white, wooly lamb. Clapping Scrooge on the shoulder, he said: "You have begun to intrigue me, sir, with this tale of yours. Never let it be said that Thaddeus Macaulay is a man without compassion, and your testimony, my dear sir, has touched me deeply." He placed a hand over his heart and blinked his eyes rapidly until a drop of moisture formed at the corners of each one.

It was perhaps the finest performance of the evening, but Scrooge was not paying much attention to it. His memory and mission regained, he knew what he had to do, but remained completely at a loss as to how to go about it. One thing however was certain: Christmas would not be saved in this drafty warehouse-cum-theatre. Gently lifting Macaulay's hand from his shoulder, he said: "Yes, yes, all very good, sir. I apologize for any inconvenience that my actions may have caused you. Now if you please, I must be about my business."

"Ah, but in the matter of your apology, sir, it is not I, your humble servant, to whom it should be directed. No sir, it is instead the young wordsmith who penned our play, who was so desperate to see its performance completed this evening. It is he of whom you must ask forgiveness, for despite the beneficial effect his work had upon you, it was you who prevented his dream of seeing his handiwork produced. I shall get him for you presently."

"But really, I must be getting on my way," Scrooge protested, unsure of exactly what way that was, but knowing that it was past eight o'clock of a Christmas Eve, it had to be traversed in short order. Thaddeus Macaulay was already bustling around his temporary domain in search of the playwright. The other actors, many having lost interest in the controversy, were quietly removing makeup and packing away props and costume pieces. "Bartholomew," Macaulay called to the actor who had played the role of Joseph Marrowbone's ghost, "have you seen our author?"

"I believe, Mr. Macaulay, he is hiding behind that crate," Bartholomew answered, peeling a cone of beeswax from his nose. Indeed, cowering in private behind a tall packing box, wishing that the floor would open up and swallow him, was the young playwright.

"Get up from there, lad," said Thaddeus Macaulay. "The excitement has ceased, it is safe to come out."

"Must I?"

"Oh, come now, get up, get up!" Grasping the collar of the young man's garment, Macaulay pulled him to his feet.

Some people wear clothes as if they were born to be in them, but the bashful, sandy-haired young writer was not among them. Instead he resembled an understudy rushed into an ill-fitting, ill-suited costume not his own. "There is a man I want you to meet," Macaulay said.

"With all due respect, sir, I really would prefer not," the playwright demurred.

Throwing an arm around the lad like a father, a role of which his life of constant travel and upheaval had robbed him, but which he had enacted on stage numerous times, Thaddeus Macaulay walked the younger man into the light. "I know what you are feeling, my boy," he began.

"I doubt that, Mr. Macaulay," the playwright said.

"Ah, but I do indeed. Think not that I was born into my present position. No, even Thaddeus Macaulay was once a young apprentice of the theatre with volumes of the acting trade yet to learn and, while I do not relate this to everyone, after my first experience treading on the boards I was as reluctant as you to show my face. But I persevered, lad, and look what has happened! You too will get over this experience. But we shall speak of that later. There is something more important I would like you to do. Talk to this old gentleman and get his story regarding the effects of your——uh, *our* play. Take down his every word, leave *nothing* out. We can always edit later." In a much smaller voice he whispered into the young playwright's ear: "That man's testimonial is gold to us, lad, *gold*."

Clapping the miserable author on the shoulder as he walked, Macaulay said gaily, "Ah, here is the fine old gentleman of whom I spoke." The writer actually closed his eyes, trying to avoid the sight of Ebenezer Scrooge. For his

112

part, Scrooge took one look at the play's author and gaped. Then with a gentle shake of his head, he laughed. "I begin to see the nature of the coincidence of this play script," he said.

"Mr. Stooge, was it not?" Macaulay said cordially, "Mr. Stooge, I would like you to meet the creator of our drama."

"How are you, Uncle Ebenezer?" young Peter Cratchit asked weakly, cracking one eye open.

"Quite well, considering," Scrooge replied, amused by the discomfort of the eldest son of his partner, Bob Cratchit.

"God's body," Thaddeus Macaulay exclaimed, "can it be that the two of you are acquainted?"

"It is a small world, is it not?" Scrooge replied.

"Well, then, it sounds as though the two of you have business to sort it out. Come friends," Macaulay called to his company, "let us repair to that excellent public house I spent some time in earlier this evening."

"And may you spend more than time this go-around," Old Ben called out.

Most of the actors did not have to be asked twice, and those few remaining members of the audience also followed Old Ben and Thaddeus Macaulay into the night and to The Twelve Bells, leaving the warehouse theatre empty except for Scrooge, Tom Bray and Peter Cratchit.

"Your father told me something about your joining a theatrical troupe as a writer, Peter," Scrooge said. "That was quite an *interesting* play."

"Are you angry, Uncle?"

"Startled, perhaps, but not angry. How could I be angry? You have given me back to myself."

"I must say, you were the last person I expected to see in the audience. Had Her Majesty herself shown up tonight, I do not think I would be in such a state of shock. How did you come to be in this place?"

113

"It is a long, strange story. But speaking of strange stories, how is that you knew of the one you borrowed for this play of yours? I never told it to you. These past seven years, I have never told a living soul about what happened to me, except for your father, so I must presume you heard the tale from him."

"How I heard it is a tale in itself," Peter said, sitting down on a crate and inviting Scrooge to do the same. Despite the anxiousness to be on his way he had exhibited mere moments before, the old man rationalized that the sudden appearance of Peter Cratchit must somehow be connected to the task ahead of him. Deciding he could spare the time in return for heightened clarity of mind, he took his seat. Tom sat on the floor nearby, like a patient dog.

"Several years ago," Peter Cratchit began, "Tim became so ill that Mother and Father were afraid he would not live through another night. They said nothing of the sort to the rest of us, but their faces betrayed their fears. I had lain awake in my bed throughout that terrible night, pretending to be asleep. In the middle of the night, Father came into the bedroom and I heard him trying to comfort Tim and himself as well. But then Tim spoke up and began telling a story, a strange story that I initially attributed to a fever dream. It was the tale of a man who traveled with ghosts on a Christmas Eve and who had been changed because of them. When he had finished, Father, who seemed not to know what to say in response, straightened Tim's blankets, kissed his feverish forehead, and started to leave the room.

"He was nearly out of the room when Tim spoke up again. "Do you not see, Father?" he said. "All this happened to Uncle Ebenezer. That is why he became a new man. If Uncle's soul can be healed by the light, so can my body. Do not worry so. I will be fine."

"Healed by the Light," Scrooge quietly echoed.

"Father left the room quickly though I heard him sobbing through the wall." Peter then paused to clear his throat and wipe something out of his eye. "From that moment on, my brother's illness ebbed away and his body strengthened. The doctor, of course, took all of the credit, but I was convinced from that night on that Tim himself, lying there in his bed, had actually *willed* his body to heal. What's more, he increasingly began to demonstrate knowledge of things and of people that go beyond his station. There is indeed a *light* about Tim now, one that burns from within. That is the only way I can describe it. Even though Father never mentioned it again, I never forgot that night long ago, or Tim's story. When Mr. Macaulay asked if I had any ideas for a Christmas pageant, I immediately began to imagine how the story could be translated to the stage. I pray you will forgive me for appropriating your past, Uncle."

"There is nothing to forgive you for," Scrooge told him. Then suddenly noticing Tom Bray, he added, "Oh, heavens, where are my manners? You have been so quiet, Tom, I nearly forgot you were there. Peter, this is Mr. Tom Bray. Tom, this is my friend, Peter Cratchit." Both men rose upon being introduced, and Peter clutched Tom's hand with the natural friendliness of all Cratchits. For his part, Tom grinned broadly and then pumped the other man's hand as if he expected water to start gushing from Peter's mouth. While conviviality with members of his own species was still something of a new experience for Tom, he was definitely getting to like it. Finally he let go of Peter's throbbing hand.

"If it were not for Tom," Scrooge went on, "I should probably still be lying in a heap out in the woods."

"In the woods? What happened to you?"

"Fell from the sky," Tom added, tracing the trajectory with one finger and landing it into his palm, as though that were all the explanation necessary.

"You fell from the sky?"

"If you believe your brother Tim's account of my transformation, sure it cannot be difficult to accept that I soared down from the heavens. I cannot recall doing so, however. My last memory was…was falling out of a coach speeding through the air."

"Have you been visited by spirits again?" Peter asked.

"Spirits are a part of the story, but there are even greater matters at hand. I have been charged with an enormous responsibility, the knowledge of which has come back to me within the last several minutes." Pulling out his watch, Scrooge noted the time with alarm. "Three-and-a-half hours is all that I have left in which to save Christmas itself," he declared. "But how in heaven's name am I to accomplish it?"

"I have no idea," Peter Cratchit said.

Scrooge sighed. "I was rather hoping you would."

"What do you mean that Christmas must be saved? Is it not nearly here?"

"I cannot explain everything now," Scrooge said. "You will simply have to put your faith in my words. But if I do not arrive at my destination by midnight, Christmas shall be no more, and the world will be cast into darkness from which it will never emerge! But I have no idea how to proceed."

"Tim would know," Peter Cratchit said. "If anyone on earth can help you, it will be he."

"Very well, but how can we get to him?" Scrooge asked, wearily.

"We will find a way, Uncle. I will help you."

Scrooge sat down on a crate. "I am suddenly so tired, so very tired. I do not know if I can make it to see Tim. Perhaps, at last, it is time to acknowledge that I have failed." A cold heaviness fell over Ebenezer Scrooge's body, and a dull ache was forming under his left arm. He closed his eyes and slowly shook his head from side to side.

"Perhaps I never had a chance." From someplace in the night, somewhere far away in the darkness, Scrooge thought he heard a low, rasping chuckle.

Placing one hand under Ebenezer Scrooge's chin, Peter Cratchit lifted it up firmly, which forced the old man to open his eyes. "Uncle Ebenezer," Peter said in a stern voice, "I have never known you to be a quitter."

Scrooge reacted as if he had been struck. Carillon had said the same thing to him one evening——and an eternity——ago, when he was about to embark on this strange journey. But he was exhausted and confused…who wouldn't be after falling down from the sky? He was also very nearly out of time. The ache in his chest was returning.

"For heaven's sake, Peter, I am only a man…a weary old man. I have not asked to be appointed the savior of Christmas and the benefactor of all Humankind. I should be sitting home by my fire, petting my cat, not gallivanting about in the burning cold and riding carriages above the clouds! It is too much! I wish to rest."

No one spoke for several moments, then Tom Bray said, with overwhelming finality, "But I want Christmas."

Scrooge looked upon the imploring face of the much younger man. "We all do, Tom, but I do not know if I can make it."

"Uncle, I will make certain you get to London and see Tim," Peter promised. "If pressed, I am sure Mr. Bray will come along, too."

Tom nodded solemnly.

"Where in heaven's name are we, anyway?" Scrooge asked.

"This village is called Pindsworth, and it is no more than two hour's ride to the City." Peter said.

"Only if we are able to engage a carriage. Do you know where we can find one?"

"No, but maybe the landlord at the pub will."

"What about your employer? He must have gotten his entire company here somehow."

"A private coach, which has since departed," Peter told him.

"Then we can do nothing," Scrooge sighed.

"The house has a coach," Tom Bray said.

"House?" Scrooge asked. "Yes, of course, the manor house! The Squire's coach! Tom, do you think he will lend it to us?"

The groom shook his head.

"He must!" Peter exclaimed.

"Tom, this is very important," Scrooge said gravely. "If Peter is right, our only chance for saving Christmas depends upon getting to London as quickly as possible. Do you understand? We must go to the Squire to ask to use his coach."

"No," Tom said. "Not him. We will ask the horses."

"The horses?" Scrooge and Peter said in unison.

Tom nodded again, but this time smiled. "They will agree."

"I have no doubt they will," Scrooge said. "Very well, let us be off." He looked around the chilly, empty warehouse. "Since it is only we three still here, I suppose I should extinguish the lanterns before we leave. I'm sure Mr. Macaulay would not appreciate being held responsible should a fire occur in this building."

Tom Bray suddenly tensed. "Stop," he said, urgently, and Peter froze in place. "Another is in here. A dark man."

"Who do you see?" Scrooge asked.

"Do not see. Feel."

Looking around the warehouse for signs of another person, and finding none, Peter Cratchit cried, "Hullo! Is anyone here?"

"Shhhhh," Tom ordered, and Peter fell silent, barely daring, in fact, to breath. The empty warehouse was eerily devoid of sound, except for a low metallic *click*.

"What was that sound?" Peter whispered.

"I do not believe that we should wait to learn what it was," Scrooge said. "We must go."

The lanterns forgotten, the three started for the door of the warehouse, with Tom in the lead, looking for danger on all sides, and Peter aiding Scrooge, who was moving with some difficulty due to a sudden lightheadedness. They had nearly made it out when Jasper Crimp lunged out from behind a stack of barrels, his hand tightly gripping a flintlock revolver.

"That man has a pistol!" Peter shouted, pulling on Scrooge's arm in an attempt to drag him to safety.

"It ends now!" Crimp cried, leveling the revolver at Scrooge and firing a shot, whose deafening explosion panicked two roosting owls in the rafters of the warehouse.

Ebenezer Scrooge cried out and fell to the floor.

TWELVE

When Jasper Crimp dashed out of the door of the warehouse, it was like fleeing directly onto the Arctic Circle. Somehow the night had become even colder. He panted as he ran and with every footfall expelled what little inner warmth he had left.

Nearly exhausted, he stopped running and leaned against a tree, hoping to catch his spent breath and try to force the cold ache in his lungs to subside. He would rest momentarily, then make his way back to his place of lodging, and after that...well, the world would be an entirely different place after that, and predicting exactly how so was beyond his capability. All Jasper Crimp knew was that he had carried out his Master's orders, which meant that his Master should be pleased enough to reward him.

That was why Jasper Crimp felt no particular fear when the Darkness descended upon him, even though it raised his level of coldness to a point where Crimp momentarily wondered if he had just died. "My lord, it is done," he said, shivering.

Is it indeeeeeeed? the voice that rode on the wind asked.

"The old man was with two others, the dumb ox and another young blighter, but they were not able to save him."

Are you certain?

Why was Lord Tenebra questioning him? Of course he had killed the old fool. He fired at close range, saw the man clutch his chest and watched him drop to the floor, while the others cried out in alarm.

"I saw it with my own eyes, my lord."

Ahhhhh, the eyes of Crimp.

There was a tone in his Master's voice that was unfamiliar to Jasper Crimp, and it was one that he did not like. Despite the night's utter frigidity, he could feel a bead of perspiration forming on his forehead. "The man is dead, my lord."

Then why do I continue to sense his consciousness? the terrible voice asked.

"I saw him fall! I heard him cry out with my own ears!"

Ahhhhh, the ears of Crimp.

Jasper Crimp slid to the ground and remained on his knees, his eyes lowered. He knew that he would not be able to see his Master even if he had wanted to anyway. He clasped his hands together and said, "My Lord Tenebra, I beg of you to give me leave to speak." When no statement of opposition came, Crimp continued. "I told you earlier this evening, my lord, that I was unskilled at murder. If the old man is still alive it is only by a thread. I beg your forgiveness for my failure. I beg it with all my heart and soul. But there is no way he will be able to accomplish his mission. There is no chance he will even make it to London."

To London...

"There was talking of taking the old fool there to see someone, but he will never survive the journey.

To see who...?

"I could not make out everything from where I was hiding, but they spoke of the brother of the new man, the young fool who was helping the old cove."

What followed was a blast of icy darkness of such extremity that Jasper Crimp was thrown onto the ground. In

121

the distance, dogs could be heard crying out in alarm and horses neighing. Crimp was unable to feel anything but black disorientation, unable even to tell whether he was facing upwards or downwards. As he lie there, frostbitten and whimpering in fear, the voice whispered as though from inside Crimp's head. *What is that man's name?* it demanded.

Jasper Crimp opened his mouth and formed the words with effort: "Cratched...I believe."

The darkness waned slightly. *Cratchit...*the voice intoned. *Tim Cratchit.*

"This person is known to you, my lord?" Crimp asked, breathing heavily and painfully.

Of course he is known to me. He is one of their agents, and a powerful one, despite his limited years. Like the old fool he has an infuriating talent for survival.

"They were planning on taking a coach from the estate of the lord of the manor house to get the old man there, but that was before I shot him."

Attempted to shoot him, Crimp.

"I attempted to *kill* him, my lord, and that was my area of failure." Crimp raised himself up from the frozen ground to a kneeling position. "I assure you there is no way the man can survive the bullet wound. He may be dead already."

He is not.

"Then allow me to finish the job, my lord. I will not fail you again. I have bullets remaining. I will kill them all this time. I will continue to serve you. Think how long I have walked in your service already."

Ahhhhh, the walking of Crimp.

"I swear to you, my lord, the old man will not live to see midnight. Let me complete my task, or else simply let him die in the coach on the way to London. Either way you will be victorious."

A long silence then followed, so long that Crimp's feeling of apprehension was developing into actual fear. "What is your decision, my lord?" he asked. "I am waiting to serve you."

Are you indeed?

"How can you question my devotion to you?"

I question your ability to succeed.

"My lord, please, if I may——"

SILENCE! the cold wind roared, and Jasper Crimp cowered under its blast. *Do you believe that you have fooled me all this time? You have no more fervent commitment to the side of the Darkness and the battle in which I am engaged than a sailor does for the captain who pressed him. You see yourself as a skilled argufier, a man who sells his ability with words to the highest bidder...a tongue for hire. When your tongue was of value to me I overlooked your weakness of faith. But you failed me this evening, Crimp, both with your tongue and your attempt at action. You are no longer of use to me.*

"You cannot kill me, my lord!" Jasper Crimp protested. "You said so yourself. It is not possible for you to take the life of a human!"

That is true...but it is possible for me to take your tongue.

Jasper Crimp opened his mouth to speak again, but no sound came out. In spite of the night's desperate cold, his tongue and throat felt like they were filled with molten rock.

What a mortal fool you are, the voice said, once more sounding as though it were coming from the inside of Crimp's brain. *Like all men you think of death as the worst possible fate. You forget punishment.*

The part of Jasper Crimp's brain that remained capable of cognizant thought attempted to order his body to flee, to run in any direction in the hopes of escaping the darkness, but when his legs finally attempted to cooperate, Crimp made it only a few feet before stopping again. Had he been able to, he would have cried out in horror as his eyes dimmed and sank into darkness.

Jasper Crimp was blind.

Frantically waving his arms about him, Crimp groped his way forward until colliding painfully with another tree and falling to the ground. A cry was stillborn in Jasper Crimp's ruined throat, and hot tears welled up in but refused to fall from his obsolete eyes.

Because of your failure, the work you began must now be finished by another of my minions. But you will not die this evening, Crimp. You will live a long life...spending every second of it wishing you had died.

An agonizing pain shot through both of Jasper Crimp's legs, a pain to which he could not acknowledge verbally. He attempted to rise from the ground, but found that he could not; his legs would not support his weight. Panicked hands ran up and down his trouser legs, hopelessly searching for the long, strong limbs that had been there mere moments earlier, but which had since been replaced by twisted, thin stubs.

What a pity it had to end this way, my oh-so-faithless servant, but you have cost me dearly, and my nature is not a forgiving one. I will take leave of you now. You shall never hear my voice again...or any other.

With that the crumpled mass that had once been Jasper Crimp, but which was now a huddled, mewling, ruined wretch of a man on an empty, freezing cold village road, was stricken deaf as well.

THIRTEEN

"Surely there is a doctor in this village, Uncle," Peter Cratchit was saying to Ebenezer Scrooge, who sat hunched and gasping on the cold floor of the warehouse. "If you cannot move, we will find him and bring him here."

"No, Peter," Scrooge panted. "I am able to move, but not to a surgery. We must be on our way."

"But Uncle, you are wounded!"

"I am ailing, Peter, but not wounded." The sharp, burning pain in his chest that had come upon him as quickly as a thrust from a bayonet was subsiding but a persistent ache remained. The sudden attack had produced one beneficial result: it had served to double Ebenezer Scrooge over at the very moment Jasper Crimp had fired his revolver, which meant the bullet had torn through the shoulder of his greatcoat, leaving his body unscathed. Crimp had fled the building not realizing that he had missed his quarry.

"Most importantly, though, I am not dead," Scrooge said, regarding his "nephew" with a knowing smile. "You are still a young man, Peter. You have not faced ailment and infirmity, and such bone-weariness that you lie in bed some evenings and wish never again to see the dawn. You have not seen the shadows in the middle of the night that beckon you to follow them, to cross over and become a shadow, too. You have not heard the voices that whisper terrible things in your ear when you are at your most vulnerable. You have not struggled against the crushing weight of a life lived mostly in the past that now bears down on the few remaining years you have left. But I will tell you one thing, my boy: there is no force on earth that has the power to remind one of the sheer worthiness of life than facing your final breath. When I beheld the revolver in that wretched man's hand and believed my time had finally come, I wished nothing more than to live. I was given that precious gift and I intend to not waste it, all my pains, ailments and frustrations be damned. Please, help me to my feet."

Each taking an arm, Tom and Peter supported Ebenezer Scrooge as he struggled to his feet.

"Uncle, are you absolutely certain that——"

"Peter," Scrooge interrupted, "the very fact that a warrior of the Darkness attempted to murder me implies I remain a danger to them. Otherwise, they would not have taken such a drastic step. That means there is still a chance of victory for the Light despite all of the obstacles thrown in our way. Therefore we must go before any more time is lost."

An eerie, blue, fog-like glow covered the country lane upon which Ebenezer Scrooge and Peter Cratchit were trotting, offering enough light for them to make out the dark shape of the brawny figure running up ahead. They were keeping apace as best they could, though each cold breath stabbed Scrooge's lungs like a dagger made of ice. Though much younger, Peter was experiencing an equal ordeal. "I can no longer feel my toes," he said. Only Tom appeared unaffected by both the cold and the exertion, running as easily and tirelessly as one of the horses he cared for, leading his friends to the grounds of Oldcastle Hall. To Peter it looked as though they were becoming hopelessly lost in the middle of a dense wood, but he struggled to keep pace, trusting the large, taciturn young man. Finally, Tom Bray stopped, offering a blessed moment of relief to his companions.

"There," Tom said, pointing to the shadow of a structure that was barely discernable, even in the mysterious, bluish luminescence that served to guide them. It was clearly not a manor house; rather a stable.

"As he said, we must ask the horses," Scrooge panted.

Tom set off again, sprinting toward the dark shadow of the stable, and Peter and Scrooge once more followed him like obedient, if frozen and exhausted, terriers. When they reached the structure, Tom motioned to them to remain silent, and then carefully unlatched the stable door and drew it as quietly as possible so as not to startle the horses. He slipped inside and motioned for Peter and Ebenezer Scrooge to follow.

The smell of horses was strong. Neither Peter nor Ebenezer Scrooge could see anything until Tom put a match to a lantern and adjusted the flame as dim as possible, just enough to wash the interior of the stable with a dull yellow glow. A half-dozen horse stalls lined one wall, only four of which were occupied, and the horses, all of which were a uniform jet black color, were asleep. Past the stalls, with only a short wall for separation was the carriage house, containing the Oldcastle family coach: large, painted garish yellow, and bearing the family crest on the doors. Going to it, Tom lifted up the front of the vehicle and pulled it out as far as space in the stable allowed. Peter Cratchit stood astounded at what should have been an impossible feat of strength for a mortal man. "What are you doing, Tom?" he whispered.

"Must hitch horses in here," the young man answered.

"He's right," Ebenezer Scrooge added. "Opening the door and taking the coach and the team out might risk drawing the attention of someone in the house, though for the life of me, I cannot see how he is going to accomplish it."

Peter could not fathom it either; while the structure was moderately large it could hardly be called spacious, particularly given the number of vehicles, animals, hay and livery equipment, and people that it now held. But just as Tom Bray had amazed him by pulling the coach out by himself, he watched with bemusement as the groom lifted, pivoted, and angled the huge vehicle around until he was satisfied with its position.

Then Tom crept to one of the stalls where an ebony horse stood sleeping with its head bowed. All Tom Bray did was lean close to it and whisper, "Up," and instantly the horse came awake. Tom gently stroked its nose, and the horse responded by nuzzling the chest of the large man. Then, as though acting under pre-arranged instructions, the steed turned its great head toward Tom and held still, as the groom whispered something more directly into its ear, his voice too quiet for either Peter or Scrooge to hear.

If what transpired next had been described to Peter Cratchit by anyone else, he might have considered that person a fool, a liar, or a drunkard. But with his own eyes Peter Cratchit saw the horse nod in agreement to Tom's words and then *smile at him*. It then stepped calmly out of the stall, stood perfectly still while Tom draped a collar around its neck, then turned and moved backwards towards the coach until it was perfectly placed for hitching. At no time did the groom touch or command the animal.

Tom repeated this same action with another of the horses, which likewise rose as meek as a lamb and did whatever quiet bidding Tom Bray wanted. Soon both were in place and standing patiently while Tom continued hitching them.

"They understand him," Peter said, awestruck. "They really understand him."

"They do," Tom agreed, deftly buckling the harness straps. It was as simple as that.

In no time the horses were ready, the other two remaining asleep and unaware in their respective stalls, and Peter and Tom jointly helped Ebenezer inside the coach.

It was nearly nine o'clock. "We cannot tarry," Scrooge told them. "Tom, I think you should drive. You do know how to drive, don't you?"

The groom nodded.

"Good. We must get to London as quickly as possible."

"Where is London?" Tom asked.

"Don't you know the way?"

Tom Bray shook his head.

"I will navigate, Uncle," Peter said. "If we can find the north road, the one past Rush Hill, then we shall have no problem getting into London, and once there I can surely direct Tom to Father's house."

"Let us be off, then," Scrooge said, climbing inside the coach and closing the door. Settling into the seat, he found himself comfortable and reasonably warm for the first time since leaving the makeshift theatre.

Peter Cratchit was about to get inside the coach as well when Tom pointed to the driver's seat and said, "No, you ride there." Before Peter could take a step Tom bodily lifted him up, practically tossing him onto the seat as though he weighed nothing.

"Tom, for heaven's sake, I can manage on my own!" Peter protested, as Tom tossed up a heavy woolen blanket, which was dirty and smelled of the horse stalls. "For the cold," Tom said, and despite its equine odor, Peter gratefully placed it over his lap.

After lighting the coach lamps, Tom put out his lantern, and without a sound and with great stealth he opened the stable doors, and ever so quietly whispered, "Go." In perfect unison the two black horses stepped off, but behind them the coach creaked and groaned loudly as it shifted and began to roll. As though conscious of the noise they were making, the horses stopped instantly in their tracks and became as statues, staying that way until "*Go*" was repeated. Very quietly, the large yellow coach rolled out, carrying Scrooge and a nervous Peter Cratchit in the

129

driver's bench, but not holding the reins. As soon as the team had cleared the doorway of the stable they halted, standing still to allow Tom Bray to close and latch the doors. He ascended to his driver's post.

"Will two horses be powerful enough for this large coach?" Peter whispered.

"They are strong," the groom replied.

"Then get us to the north road, Tom. I will direct you from there."

Once more the groom whispered, "Go," though this time his voice was so soft that Peter was not certain he heard him; the horses, however, did. They began to move in careful slow steps. The vehicle wheeled past the foot of the carriage drive that ran to the hall, traveling slowly and quietly, so quietly in fact that Peter judged the pounding of his own heart to be louder than the footfalls of the horses. They were almost past the carriage drive and the manor house when a sudden shriek high overhead pierced the night stillness, startling both the horses and riders.

Like an avenging demon, an enormous falcon swooped out of the sky and passed over the heads of the horses, raking the mane of one of them with its talons. "What was that?" Peter Cratchit demanded as the falcon circled up, then dived again, screeching as it descended and beating the faces of the team with its wings. The frightened horses shied and whinnied and Tom whispered sharply, "Hush!" but for once his voice had no effect on the animals. The falcon continued to hover about them, battering their heads with its cruel wings and reaching for their eyes with its claws until the horses reared up in fear.

From inside the coach Scrooge called: "What is happening?"

"We are being attacked by a falcon!" Peter cried.

"Not a falcon," Tom said, puzzled by this creature that looked like a falcon but did not act like one. As he watched the bird swooping over the frightened horses, Tom realized that, for the first time in his life, he too was afraid of a creature of nature.

"Can't you strike at it, Tom?" Scrooge shouted, and at the sound of his voice the falcon stopped its attack and flew over to the window of the coach, in front of which it hovered unnaturally in midair like a hummingbird, glaring at Ebenezer with unnaturally glowing yellow eyes. "Great God," Scrooge cried in sudden realization, "that is no falcon, it is one of them!"

"One of whom?" Peter shouted back.

"One of the minions of Tenebra! He has somehow invaded the body of a bird of prey!"

"Who is Tenebra?"

"Our enemy, Peter, the one we have been fighting."

"House!" Tom cried, and both Peter and Scrooge turned their attention to the manor house, which up until then had been all but hidden in the darkness of the night. Now lights appeared in a window.

"We have been detected!" Peter said. "Tom, we must leave now!"

But the groom's hands were full trying to control the horses under the onslaught of the falcon-creature, which had resumed its attack on them, beating them about the ears and scratching at their faces with its claws and beak. Taking up the whip that lay beside him Peter Cratchit lunged out at the bird, trying to drive it away, but the falcon maddeningly darted just out of his reach.

"Someone is coming," Scrooge called out, as voices were heard coming from the house. The coach bucked back and forth as the horses reared, whinnying loudly as they attempted to fight back with their hooves, but the owl merely circled once more, and then swooped down again, tearing at the ear of one. "That thing will blind the horses if it gets the chance! We must kill it!" Peter cried.

The dim outlines of two men, one very tall and lean and the other short, round and agitated, could now be seen rushing from the house towards the coach. "Who is out there? What are you doing?" the piping voice of Squire Oldcastle squealed. "Thieves, I shouldn't wonder! Stop, stop I say! Osmund, after them!"

A third figure then joined them, also short and round, and wearing a nightgown and head kerchief; it was Lady Oldcastle, who shouted, "What on earth is going on out here! Mortimer, get inside immediately! It is no night to be out!"

"We are being robbed, Matilda!" he called back.

Holding the reins with one hand, Tom Bray grabbed the whip away from Peter Cratchit and slashed the air, missing the bird by a fraction of an inch. He lashed out at the demonic creature again and cried in frustration as he accidentally struck one of the horses, which bolted forward several feet before he was able to rein it in.

"Tom, for God's sake, hurry!" Scrooge called, as the two figures ran down the carriage drive from the house towards them.

Something was happening to Tom Bray, something that he had never experienced before and something he did not like. He felt hot and confused, but strong——very strong——and the need to use that strength all but overpowered him. His head spun, and he suddenly wanted to hurt the owl. He *wanted* to!

For the first time in his life Tom Bray felt hate.

Baring his teeth and emitting a low growl, he made a desperate lunge, the whip now an extension of his body, and he brought it down as hard as he could on the falcon's head. With a startled cry the bird dropped down between the team, landing with a thud, barely able to get out of the way of the horses' hooves, which clomped down around it, trying to crush it. The screeching bird fluttered out from under the horses, and just as suddenly as it had appeared, it flew off into the night. And as it sped away, weakened and clumsy from its injury, Tom saw that it was a falcon after all. Only a falcon, with normal avian eyes. He had lashed out in hatred and hurt a living creature.

"I don't want to hurt things," Tom said morosely.

"You didn't hurt that falcon so much as you knocked the devil out of it," said Scrooge. "But I'm afraid we are in for more trouble."

"Stop you thieves, you blackguards! Stop I say!" hollered Squire Oldcastle, who was huffing and puffing as he neared the coach, with only Osmund behind him, Lady Oldcastle had since retreated to the warmth of the manor. "I shall see you hang for this!" the Squire shouted as he approached the coach, "every last one of you!" Turning to the servant, he demanded: "You lout, get those men down from there! Use force if you have to!"

Holding onto the lantern, Osmund sprinted ahead of the Squire and, employing the gait of a marathon runner, reached the coach within seconds. Casting his light on the driver, Osmund looked into the guilty face of the stable groom. "Tom, what are you doing up there?"

"Must go to the city, to London," the groom replied.

Turning his light toward Peter Cratchit, Osmund asked: "And who might you be?"

"I might as well be a convicted housebreaker, for all the trouble I have managed to get us into," Peter said glumly.

"Whoever you robbers are, I will make certain you rot in Newgate prison!" the Squire decried.

"I do not understand what is happening," Osmund said, but Scrooge beckoned to him from the door of the coach. The servant shined the light inside the coach, and cried: "You!"

"Yes, and this is all my doing," Scrooge said, "so please do not blame Tom. I assure you that I am not in the thievery trade, and will be more than happy to provide recompense for any damage or inconvenience, but this is a matter of life and death, more than you can possibly imagine. I cannot explain further right now except to say that it is imperative that we get to London as soon as possible. I beg of you to believe me!" As he spoke, Scrooge prayed that Peter Cratchit's insight was correct, that Tim Cratchit would be able to help him.

Instead of commenting further Osmund threw the lantern to the ground and propelled himself headfirst through the window of the coach, shouting: "Help! Help! Let me go, you villain! Help! My lord, please help me!"

"What are you doing?" Scrooge asked in alarm as Osmund fought mightily against an invisible force.

In the midst of this great struggle the servant whispered, "Nothing more than trying to make this look good for the benefit of my master. I have no idea what you are up to, Mr. Plummet, though I personally wish to help since your appearance here has resulted in more genuine delight to me than I can recall in a quinquennial." Then for the benefit of his employer outside he shouted, "Leave me alone, you brute!" In a hushed voice he continued: "As you require the use of this vehicle, we must make this abduction of the master's property as convincing as possible, eh? I do hope you understand. *OUCH*! *Stop that, you heathen*!" The servant kicked and flailed his limbs as though fending off the forces of Hell itself, then whispered to Scrooge: "Go and do what you must do, sir, and do not worry, I shall take care of things here. A pleasant journey to you, Mr. Plummet."

"Actually, my name is Scrooge."

"In that case, best to you, Mr. Scrooge." Then in tones of anguish, Osmund cried, "*Oh, will no one help me*?"

"I am here, I am coming!" the Squire said, having summoned up the necessary courage and declared himself of a mind to rescue his manservant from the terrible force within the coach, whatever it was. "Let my man go, you...you...you *fiend*!" Squire Oldcastle shouted as he grasped the heron legs of the servant, still kicking madly through the window while the upper half of him remained swallowed up by the coach.

With growing alarm, Tom threw down the reins and prepared to jump from the driver's seat, but Peter, who had heard the conversation between his "uncle" and the flailing servant stopped him. "No, no, don't go down, Ebenezer is fine. They are pretending, Tom, like actors in a play."

"Play," Tom repeated, smiling.

On the ground, Squire Oldcastle wrapped his arms tightly around Osmund's legs and braced his foot against the bottom of the coach. "I shall save you, but you will owe me for this!" he said, then pulled with all his might. At that moment, Osmund released his hold on the door and master and servant flew backwards and tumbled to the dirt, a heap with eight limbs waving madly in the air like an overturned beetle.

"Go, Tom, *now!*" Scrooge shouted and this time the team sprang into action, pulling the coach ahead so suddenly that Scrooge was driven into the back of the seat from the force. But at long last, they were off.

"All will be well now, Uncle!" Peter Cratchit called down, optimistically.

"Will it?" Scrooge muttered as he sank into the upholstery, physically and mentally exhausted. He remembered a time earlier in his life when he would go for nights on end without sleep, poring over books and ledgers and accounts, unable to stop for rest or even food until he had tracked down an error that meant only a penny's difference in his wealth. But even in the worst of times he had never felt so bone-tired and spent as he did at this moment. *Damn my former life*, he thought, bitterly. The unfortunate memory of it only served to deepen a gnawing melancholy that he was too tired to fight off: an entire lifetime wasted in the pursuit of money and property that would still remain in the world long after he had gone, in someone else's pockets or on someone else's ledger books.

If only his redemption had come sooner. If only he could have gotten an earlier start, how much more might he have been able to accomplish.

His heart began to pound and ache once more, and he clutched his closed fist to his chest. He was tired; God in Heaven, so tired. "Please...somebody...please help me," he begged, closing his eyes and allowing his head to slump onto his chest.

At that moment something light and soft and wonderful touched his brow, and a pleasant, musical voice said: "Feeling poorly, dear brother?"

*That voice...*her *voice!*

A warm hand continued to caress his face as he opened his eyes and saw the young woman seated across from him, radiating a soft, beautiful light. There was a comforting smile on her pleasing face. "My poor Ebenezer," she said.

"Fan?" he whispered weakly. "How now, is that you? Heavens, how can this be? Fan, oh Fan!" Tears sprung from his eyes at the sight of his long-since-departed sister, and he reached out to embrace her. It was like holding air. "Oh, Fan, you are still young and beautiful! You are exactly as you were before you——" He stopped suddenly, not wanting to speak the word. How long *had* it been since his sister died, losing her own life in the act of bringing her son Fred into the world? It was as long as he had walked the earth without anyone to love.

"I am as I was, dear brother," she answered.

"But I am old, Fan; old, withered, and used up. Just look at me."

"I am looking, Ebenezer, and what I see is what I have always seen, a man of decency, goodness, and nobility. Little has changed."

"Much has changed, dear Fan. So much. There have been times when I've felt like a wind uncertain of which direction to blow. Oh, Fan, you have come back to me.

Except for you, I don't believe I have ever loved another person."

"Oh, tosh. What of that boy, Tim, whom you love as though he were your own grandson?"

"Well, yes, I suppose all the Cratchit children have become dear to me," Scrooge admitted. Then he looked up at her, a puzzled expression on his face. "But how could you know of Tim? He was born long after you...you..."

"The word is *died*, Ebenezer, and I am far beyond carrying any fear of it. I have watched over you. I have seen the way you have given of yourself to the Cratchit family and those other families to whom you have opened your home. I have seen you worrying over that young boy who lives beneath you, ensuring that he and his family have enough food and clothing. I have even seen you doting over that silly cat of yours to whom you gave my name...really!" She slapped his knee in mock, loving indignation.

Ebenezer Scrooge smiled at the mention of the calico, but it faded quickly. "If you have seen all that, Fan, then you have also seen the wretched man that I once was, the cold, heartless miser who nearly let Tim Cratchit die before acting to save him. I was nearly too late."

"In matters of love, it is never too late. Tim Cratchit lives today because of the care you brought to him and his family."

"But the boy's own brother has told me he managed to heal himself."

"Look at me, Ebenezer."

Scrooge looked up into the perfect, kind face he remembered so well from his youth.

"For a time you allowed yourself to be led astray by the love of wealth," Fan said, gently, "and for that you continue to torture yourself."

"I do so because I was such a fool," Scrooge said, shaking his head sadly. "Money became the love of my life, driving away all rivals, even my poor Elizabeth, who released me from my commitment of marriage when she realized that she could never compete with my affection for gold." Scrooge was unable to keep a tear from forming in his eye as he hoped the young woman he once loved and had allowed to leave more than two-score years earlier, had managed to have a life happier than any he could have given her.

Fan reached out and put a hand to his lips, a sensation that felt like being kissed by the lightest of spring breezes. "You must let the past be past, Ebenezer," she said. "You have returned to your first love, your truest love, the greatest love of your life, and that is the only thing that is important."

"What is the love of which you speak?"

"Your love of humanity, dear brother."

"Oh, my darling Fan, I wish I could believe that," he sighed, "but for years I denied humanity, including my own. I lived as a machine, separating myself from others as completely as I could, loving as little as possible, even eating as little as possible, as if I were not human at all but some kind of mill. That is what I was, Fan, a machine for milling money out of misery."

Fan remained silent for a few moments, and then asked: "What do you remember of father, Ebenezer?"

"What *don't* I remember of him?" Scrooge replied. "A worldly man if ever there was one, a harsh man. He never liked me."

"Even now, you cannot see. It was not *you* he disliked, Ebenezer. It was the great love that he saw inside of you that became the object of his scorn. There is so much you do not remember about yourself, your compassion, your caring for others. It was that very compassion that Father could not abide, because he had none himself. You know that Father always hated what he could not possess. He tried to whip that love out of you, force you to suppress that compassion and channel your attention into material concerns."

"I remember him telling me he would only acknowledge me as his son if I became a success in business," Scrooge said. "I only wanted to please him."

"He turned you against yourself, brother, at least for a while. But what you never knew was that, like you, he later experienced a change of heart. Only when he saw what you had become, saw the kind of man he had managed to create, did he realize his own grievous failing. He died drowning in a sea of regret."

"Dear God," Scrooge uttered, "I had no idea."

"That is why you must bury the past. You cannot allow yourself to succumb to the same fate. Forget what you were; acknowledge only what you *are*. I know your body has become weary, but you are not finished, no matter what your body, your mind, or *anything else* might whisper to you in the dead of night. It is not yet time for you to go. There is still a purpose for you. I know your task is difficult, dear Ebenezer. It is a terrible responsibility, but you must continue to bear it." She reached over and lovingly took Scrooge's thin face in her gossamer hands, and the warmth of her eyes filled him. "You must not become consumed by the past you cannot change. You must think only of the future...which you *can*. I must go now, Ebenezer, my time is up. Goodbye, my darling brother."

"Fan, oh, don't leave me again, Fanny dear, don't——"

Looking around him, Ebenezer Scrooge saw that he was once again alone, assuming, that is, that his sister had been there in the first place and had not simply been another phantom of the mind. He closed his eyes and slumped against the side of the coach, remaining there until a violent bump jolted him. For a moment it seemed that the coach was on the verge of overturning. Ebenezer Scrooge could hear the voice of Peter Cratchit calling out in alarm.

Sliding the window down, he stuck his head out into the night and called up: "What is happening?"

"I don't know," Peter called back. "It felt as though we ran over something."

Slowly and roughly, the coach came to a tilting stop. Tom Bray leapt down from the driver's seat and quickly circled the coach, inspecting it. "No," he cried.

"What is it?" Scrooge asked, climbing out of the coach. Peter Cratchit also came down from his seat and the two of them rushed to where Tom Bray was standing. Illumination provided by the coach lanterns allowed all three men saw the cause of their stoppage, and, for Ebenezer Scrooge, the cruel end of his mission. A large fallen tree branch had become entwined in the yellow spokes of one back wheel, splintering its spokes. As a result the wheel was rendered useless, and the coach immovable.

"Dear God," Scrooge uttered as he surveyed the ruined wheel, a ball of ice forming in the pit of his stomach. "That is it, then, we have lost."

FOURTEEN

"Darkness shall reign forever because of a tree limb," Scrooge said ruefully. "I cannot believe it."

"You cannot give up all hope, Uncle," Peter Cratchit said. "We will find another way to London. Tom, unhitch the horses and we can ride there."

"Please, Peter," Scrooge said, "a journey of two hours on horseback would be the end of me. At best you would be delivering my corpse to your brother, which I do not believe would help anyone."

"There must be some way!"

Tom Bray stood silent and attentive and raised his hand to prevent the other two from speaking. After a moment, he said: "Someone is coming."

Peter Cratchit could hear nothing, but he had come to trust Tom's senses. "Another carriage?" he asked.

The groom nodded.

"Perhaps we can persuade the driver to take us on our journey," Peter cried.

Out of the dark night a piping voice could be heard, one that carried over the sounds of the hoof beats: "Can't you make this thing go any faster, constable?"

"I would not put much reliance on the prospect of assistance, Peter," Scrooge uttered, recognizing the voice.

"Him," was all Tom Bray said.

The carriage was now coming into view out of the darkness, a simple black coach pulled by a white horse. The owner of the voice heard from afar was thrust half-out of the window on one side, and continued to yell: "I see it! I see the coach! Stop you blackguards, you thieves, you criminals! Hurry, man! Can't you spur your nag on?"

Squire Oldcastle had arrived in a police wagon.

"We shall be sent to prison!" Peter cried in alarm. "We must away!"

"How, my boy?" Scrooge asked.

The constable driving the wagon, a sturdy man with a thick, rapidly freezing moustache, leapt down from his seat.

"Arrest them!" the Squire shouted, nearly falling as he stepped out of the wagon. "Arrest them all!"

"I'll take it from here, if you don't mind sir," P.C. Worthing told him. He then shined a lantern light on the face of Peter Cratchit. "You recognize this one, guv?"

"I have never seen that man prior to this night, but what matter is that? It is not as though I habitually associate with criminals and robbers! Arrest the man, I say."

"Constable," Peter began, "I believe I can explain this entire unfortunate situation, if you would offer me the chance."

"Explain!" the Squire exploded, "there is nothing to explain, except that you nearly killed my servant and stole my coach! Explain, indeed! You and your confederate Tom Bray will spend the rest of your life in leg irons! Constable, do your duty and arrest them, and be quick about it, man, before I freeze like an icicle!" The Squire then retreated back inside the police carriage and slid the window up against the cold.

Constable Worthing trained the light from his lantern on Tom, who was standing as still as a statue. "Is this one Bray?" he asked.

"Indeed, the scoundrel! That is my stable groom. My *former* stable groom!"

"So he's the one behind this theft?"

"Bray? God's breath, man, don't be an imbecile! Tom Bray has not the brains of a newborn calf! He could not plot such a deed."

"Who did, then?" the constable asked.

"The responsibility for this act resides within me, constable," Ebenezer Scrooge said, and the unseen presence of a third suspect so startled the provincial policeman that he nearly dropped his lantern. "These two young men are blameless, and should not be charged. I am the one who necessitated transport to London. They simply sought to help me."

"By stealing this coach?"

"Not stolen," Tom Bray said.

"Is that a fact? Who, then, gave you permission? The squire here? His servant?"

"The horses."

Constable Worthing opened and closed his mouth, but no sound came out.

Pushing the carriage window back down, Squire Oldcastle called out: "What are you doing out there? Why haven't you arrested them?"

Worthing sighed heavily as he mentally challenged the wisdom of his decision to join the county constabulary. He was tired, he was cold, and he was growing weary of being harangued by the local noble. "Look, blokes," he said to the would-be coach-nappers, "I don't want any trouble tonight. It's just too blinkin' cold. So do us a favor and just stay where you are for a bit longer."

"Constable," Ebenezer Scrooge said, leaning out of the coach window, "may I have a word?"

Worthing cast his light onto Scrooge and then called back to Squire Oldcastle, "There's a third 'un in here, guv. You didn't tell me there were three."

"What difference does it make?" the Squire responded. "Arrest them all and be quick about it!"

143

The policeman sighed yet again. "Look, sir, one bloke I could handle by myself. Two would be a bit of a problem, particularly as this one's as big as a tree. But three...that's a tall order for one country peeler, even when the third one's an older bloke."

"And older bloke, you say? The brains of this rag-tag outfit, no doubt! Another Fagin, I shouldn't wonder! A veritable lord of crime here within your very grasp! Certainly Bray is not capable of planning such a brazen act, and that other fellow looks too much like a spaniel to convince me of his criminality. Ha! Bring forth the ringleader of this pack of thieves! Drag him here and let me see him!"

"Yes sir." Motioning for Ebenezer Scrooge to get out of the coach, Constable Worthing escorted him to the police wagon and then illuminated his face with the lantern. "Here he is, guv."

Looking into the face of Ebenezer Scrooge caused Squire Oldcastle to gasp. Even squinting and grimacing under the glare of the lantern, the old man's identity was unmistakable. Sweat broke out on his brow. "What are you trying to do, constable, make a fool of me?" he demanded.

"Here now!"

"The world has indeed gone mad!" the Squire shouted. "That is the only explanation! Why in heaven's name are you wasting my time with this man? This man does not exist!"

"Come again, sir?"

"He...does...not...exist," the Squire repeated slowly, as though talking to an infant only learning to speak. "Am I the only one who possesses enough rationality to grasp that that man there is not really *there*?"

"Are you feeling all right, guv?"

"Of course! There is nothing wrong with me, but if you cannot recognize a man who does not exist when you see

144

him, then it is you who are a candidate for the asylum! I have half-a-mind to take this up with your superiors!"

"I wish you'd locate the other half," Constable Worthing muttered, wondering if he had managed to blunder his way into a congregation of escaped lunatics.

"What? What did you say to me?" the Squire shouted.

"Squire Oldcastle, you called me out into this freezing night to chase your coach, which you said was stolen."

"It was stolen! And my servant was attacked and beaten within an inch of his life!"

"Right." Turning his attention to Peter Cratchit, Constable Worthing asked: "Afore God, man, did you beat that servant?"

"I did not," Peter replied.

Turning to Tom Bray, the only one of the three suspects who looked even capable of besting another man in a fight, he repeated the question. Tom vigorously shook his head.

"Right. How 'bout you, then, grandfather?"

"I have never laid a finger on a man in a physical altercation in my life," Ebenezer Scrooge answered, content in the knowledge that Peter, Tom and he were speaking the absolute truth: Osmund had faked the attack, which any cursory examination of his person by a physician would have uncovered through his lack of bruises and abrasions.

"Of *course* he did not attack my servant!" Squire Oldcastle asserted. "How many times must I say it? That man does not exist! Why do you insist upon wasting all our time by examining a witness who is not there?"

"Right," the constable said, stroking his iced moustache. "That's it, then. I've had about enough of this. I'm frozen through and this investigation is over. Go on, the lot of you. Everybody get on home."

With a shout of outrage the Squire jumped out of the police carriage, pulled himself to his full height, and confronted, eye-to-eye, the second brass button on the

145

constable's coat. "You mean you are going to do nothing with these blackguards?" the Squire shouted. "Have you taken leave of your senses? There has been a capital crime committed!"

Constable Worthing viewed the man with a stare every bit as cold as the night air. "By your own testimony, that man there don't exist, right?"

"Yes, and I *still* say so!"

"Right. And this coach was taken in the first place so the man what don't exist could get himself to London."

"Well, he did say——"

"Right," the constable interrupted. "So what we got here is a crime that was committed on the behalf of a man who don't exist. Therefore, guv, *the crime don't exist either*! You called me out to recover your coach, and there she is. Now, since my constabulary purview does not extend to the vicinity of Bedlam, I wash my hands of the lot of you!"

"How dare you speak to me in such a manner!" Squire Oldcastle cried. "You watch yourself, my good man, or I shall...I shall..."

But Constable Worthing was already in the seat of his carriage. With a snap of the reins, the steed bolted, and the sounds of the police vehicle speeding away could be heard in counterpoint to the Squire's increasingly squeaking torrent of threats. At last he gave up, uttering: "You see before you the most put upon man in the Empire."

"Sir," Peter Cratchit said, shivering, "a more immediate problem faces us."

"Why should this be so, you ask?" the squire continued, even though no one had asked. "I shall tell you. It is because of *him*!" He thrust a stubby finger toward Tom Bray. "My fate was sealed the very day this whelp arrived at our house!"

For his part, Tom Bray simply looked at the Squire with an uncomprehending frown on his face.

"Oh, what is the use?" the Squire said. "I can no longer feel my toes in this blasted cold. Let us be away from this place. Bray, you will drive, but I warn you: the moment we arrive back at the manor, you are banished from its premises. I never wish to see you again!"

"Leaving here will be difficult, I fear," Ebenezer Scrooge said, his voice heavy with resignation.

"And why would that be so?" the Squire blurted before realizing that he was responding to the figure he did not believe existed. Reacting with horror upon the realization, he quickly turned to Peter and repeated the question.

"One of the rear wheels is broken," the young man answered.

"So you have added vandalism to your list of crimes?" the Squire shouted. "How do you propose that I get to my home you miscreant malefactor?"

"Walk," Tom Bray replied.

"Oh, fine! That is all well and good for you. You are used to living in the wilderness like a white hart! I am not. Walk, indeed! If I stay out in this frigid night much longer, I shall freeze solid!"

"Since you seem predisposed to disavow your senses," Ebenezer Scrooge offered, "perhaps you should refuse to believe that the cold exists."

"I shall brook no insolence from you, sir," Squire Oldcastle rejoined. "I would not do so even if you were there."

"Wait," Tom Bray said, silencing his companions. With his head held high as though smelling the air, he added: "Horses."

"Where?" Peter asked.

"Coming this way."

"Is the constable returning?" Scrooge asked.

"It is the director of an asylum, I shouldn't wonder," the Squire said under his breath.

Within moments the sound of hooves clattering down on the hard road could be heard and a second later, the faint yellow glare of a carriage lamp shone through the darkness. A white shape could be seen emerging from the darkness: a stallion the color of snow. Tom Bray stared intently as the animal approached them, pulling behind it an enclosed hansom cabriolet, whose driver reined in the ivory steed to a halt in front of the men. Tom continued to study the animal, which appeared to study him back, but Scrooge was more interested in the driver: a man in an Ulster coat and a short top hat…it was the driver who had sped him through the night sky, attempting to deliver him to the Tribunal of the High Justice!

"Evenin' sir," the driver bade, tipping his hat. "You've not been an easy one to find."

"It is you!" Ebenezer Scrooge cried jubilantly. "Thank heaven! All is not lost! There is still time!"

"Aye, sir, though not much," the cabman said. "We needs be on our way."

"Indeed we must," the Squire said, stepping up onto the foot tread of the hansom and listing it. "Oldcastle Hall, and be quick about it." Then he clambered inside.

Now Peter Cratchit rushed up to the front of the cab, shouting, "No, no, we must get to London as quickly as possible!"

"We are not going to London, you lunatic!" the Squire shouted.

"I *know* where we are going, gents," the cabman said with startling authority and force. "We are taking a direct route, and it only involves him." He pointed his whip at Ebenezer Scrooge. "You sir," he said to Peter, "kindly step away, your uncle is in good hands."

"My uncle," the young man repeated, "how do you know that is my private name for him?"

"Peter, please do as he requests," Scrooge said. "He is speaking the truth. I know this man. At least I assume he is a man and not a spirit."

"A traveler, sir," the cabman replied, "like yourself."

"Yes, they must go," Tom Bray said, gently stroking the white horse on the blaze, and the horse responding to his words with what appeared to be a nod of agreement.

"Oh, I see," Peter Cratchit said finally, "this man is one of *them*."

That having been settled, the cabman then opened the trapdoor at the top of the hansom and barked: "You down there, remove yourself."

"I will do no such thing!" Squire Oldcastle replied, crossing his arms as best he could over his jacketed girth. "I insist you take me to my home."

"Blimey," the cabman spat, climbing down from the driver's seat and facing the Squire directly. "We got no time for this," he said. "Where we're going, you're not allowed, now be off with you!"

"I refuse to move, you scoundrel!"

At that moment a gust of cold wind blew through the coach, and riding on it was a low, ominous, rattling laugh. *Stay where you aaaaaare...* said a voice that only Squire Oldcastle seemed able to hear. "What was that?" he demanded. "Who spoke?"

Now the cabman was clutching the squire's sleeve, trying to bodily pull him out of the hansom, while Tom and Peter watched in puzzlement at what was transpiring. "You sir," he called to Ebenezer Scrooge, "go ahead and get in. As soon as I pull this lump of suet out, we'll be on our way."

"I will see up the dock, you highwayman!" the Squire shouted, and again the laugh returned to his ears.

At that moment the quiet of the desolate, wooded road shattered and a shrill screech filled the ears of everyone, startling even the cabman. "It is back!" Tom Bray cried, pointing up at a shape that was rapidly descending upon them. It was the enormous, fiery-eyed falcon that had attacked them earlier. With an angry screech, it swooped down over the head of the cabman, knocking off his hat, then circled up again and dived once more, this time raking its talons over the back of his high-collared coat forcefully enough to throw the man to his knees. Picking up a nearby rock, Tom lobbed it at the night bird, who easily soared out of the way.

"Uncle, get inside for your own protection!" Peter Cratchit hollered, and Scrooge stepped into the hansom, just as the circling owl came back for another attack. This time it grazed the ears of the white horse, who reared in alarm and then bolted, galloping driverless down the dark country road, pulling behind it the hansom containing Ebenezer Scrooge and Squire Oldcastle.

Rushing to the cabman on the ground, Peter Cratchit asked, "Are you hurt?"

"No, not hurt, but I have failed!" the man replied. "Without a strong driver of the Light, who knows where that cab will end up?"

Tom Bray watched the two-wheeled vehicle rattle its way into the darkness until it was nearly gone, and then shouted three words, following them with a rare laugh. Then he went after the hansom, chasing it into the night.

"Blimey," the cabman said, rising from the ground, "there still might be a chance. That fellow might be a traveler without his realizing it. What was it he said before dashing off?"

"I cannot not certain," Peter Cratchit replied, "but it sounded like, 'Two against one.'"

"Two against one," the cabman echoed quietly. "Here, my friend, help me unhitch these horses from that fat blighter's coach. If we're careful we can ride them back to his house."

Because of all of the strange happenings and arguments over what existed in reality and what did not, Peter Cratchit had all but forgotten about the midnight team, who were now standing as still as twin stone guards in front of an ancient temple...or else frozen to the ground. As it turned out, the former was the truth, and the steeds snapped to life as soon as the cabman approached them and deftly disconnected them from the vehicle hitch.

"What do we do once we have arrived there?" Peter asked, looking skeptically on the prospect of mounting the enormous animal without the safety of a saddle, stirrups, and reins, and remaining on her back for the distance to Oldcastle manor.

The cabman looked up at the night sky. "All we can do is pray they are successful," he said. "The rest is out of our hands now."

FIFTEEN

The hansom cab pulled by the lightning-white horse raced up the country road like the devil himself was driving, violently jostling both Ebenezer Scrooge and Squire Oldcastle, though only the latter responded verbally, issuing a series of yips and squeaks and frightened gasps. Then as mysteriously as the horse had bolted, its pace dropped from a full Ascot gallop to a gentle canter.

"Perhaps the steed has grown weary," Scrooge said, grateful that the wild bucking and bouncing of the cab had ceased, sparing his aching body and burning chest the additional aggravation. "That or it has become lost."

Squire Oldcastle said nothing. His round head retreated into the collar of his coat like a turtle's retracting into its shell.

"Perhaps one of us should attempt to take the reins," Scrooge suggested. "I must confess, though, that I am not much of a horseman."

At last, the Squire moaned, "Why do you torment me so?"

"I beg your pardon?"

"What have I ever done to you that I should deserve this?"

"It is certainly not my intention to give you cause for grievance."

"And yet you do, sir; you do!" the Squire said, before sinking once more into an uncomfortable silence.

The white horse had come to a complete halt and was hoofing the ground as though unsettled, and it was at that moment that Scrooge felt the weight of a man on the back of the hansom. "Is someone up there?" he called out, and above him the trapdoor opened up, revealing a face, which Scrooge could only barely make out in the dim light. "Tom!" he shouted.

"What? Who?" the Squire inquired. "Bray, is that you out there?"

"Me," Tom Bray called back, no more winded than a deer for having run through the woods in order to catch up with the carriage. As soon as the groom took the reins, the horse calmed itself and stood still, awaiting its command.

"Has the cabman come with you?" Scrooge asked.

"The hat man?"

"Yes, yes, the fellow who was driving this cab, is he up there with you?"

"No, only Tom."

Ebenezer Scrooge pounded his fist into the seat beside him, which jostled and startled the Squire. "One foot forward, two furlongs back," Scrooge said. "What good is the carriage without the driver?"

"Tom will drive," the groom called back.

"But you have no idea where it is I must go!"

"The horse knows."

Squire Oldcastle, who had remained silent for the last few minutes, now placed his thumb and forefinger on each side of his nose and pinched it until he cried out in pain.

"What in heaven's name are you doing?" Scrooge asked him.

"Trying to force myself to awaken from this pernicious nightmare!" the Squire replied. "I am seated in a strange, cramped, vehicle being piloted by an imbecile who communicates with horses, in the company of a man who does not exist. This is no doubt the result of that additional draught of porter I consumed after dinner."

"I wish I could convince you of the reality of this situation, but I suppose there is little use," Scrooge said, as the hansom started up again. "I daresay, though, that arriving at our final destination may be something of a shock for you."

"I care not what you daresay," the Squire said, closing his eyes and leaning back in the seat.

The cab was picking up speed steadily and yet at once it ceased to bounce over the rough road; the sound of the hoof beats quieted as well. Ebenezer Scrooge said, as he leaned forward to look through the window of the hansom. Once what he saw would have shocked him into silence, but at that moment it instead gave him a sense of joy. He knocked on the trapdoor above him and waited for Tom Bray to open it. "You were right, Tom, the horse does know the way!" he cried. "But hold the reins tightly nevertheless!"

"Whatever are you shouting about," the Squire groused. "Whatever it is, stop it at once."

"As you wish. Though I think you may want to open your eyes and view the scenery around us."

Squire Oldcastle cocked one eye open and tentatively turned his broad head toward the window at the side...then he screamed. "What...? How...? Dear God in Heaven!" he shouted.

"Lovely, isn't it?" Scrooge asked, savoring the sight of the tall tree tops, which were now even with the bottom of the cab, which was soaring upwards through the air! The white steed continued to gallop mightily, but since there was nothing solid beneath its hooves, it did so silently. Similarly the two wheels of the cab continued to spin, even though the road was now so far below them that it disappeared into the darkness. Ahead of them, like a beacon, was the moon...half of which was light, while the other half was bathed in darkness. *How appropriate*, Scrooge thought.

"God's breath!" the Squire gasped, grasping onto the seat for dear life, even though he was in no serious danger as long as he remained seated within the cab. "What is the meaning of this?"

"Have you never wondered why they call a vehicle such as this a *fly*?" Scrooge said, following the comment with a hearty, if painful laugh.

"This...cannot...be!"

"It can. It is. At long last, I am on my way to my destination and with Tom on the sprung seat I believe I will make it this time."

"You have mentioned the destination twice," the Squire said in a voice as small as a frightened mouse's squeak. "*Where* are we going?"

"To the final judgment."

Any color that may have graced the face of Mortimer Oldcastle faded away and his head fell back against the seat. He remained so motionless that for a moment Scrooge worried that the man might have died of fright right in front of him. But then the staring eyes blinked and the Squire uttered: "This is it, then."

"This is what?"

"The moment I have dreaded this score of years. It was foolish to believe I would be able to escape; madness, I shouldn't wonder."

"Escape what?"

"My day of judgment and of retribution."

"*Your* day?"

"Please, sir, you do not have to keep up the pretense any longer. I now know who you are and I know why you have been sent."

"You do?"

"Of course. What other explanation is there? My time is over, and you have been sent to fetch me and bring me to my eternal reward. And it will not go easily for me, I fear, not at all." The Squire's bloated figure appeared to deflate.

155

"I have lived with the dreadful secret all these years, and what has it gained me?"

Ebenezer Scrooge stared back at his carriage mate. "Forgive me, but what dreadful secret is that?"

"Oh, please drop the pretense of ignorance. It does not become you. You, of course, know of what I speak since you have been sent to claim me for final judgment."

All of this made little sense to Scrooge whose problems and challenges this night did not, to his knowledge, include having been sent to claim anybody.

"I imagine that a confession must be heard for me to have any chance at redemption," the Squire said, dejectedly.

Since there was not much else he could do while waiting to arrive at the High Tribunal, Scrooge agreed to listen.

With a heavy sigh, Squire Mortimer Oldcastle opened the dark, locked box that had been hidden inside his soul most of his life, and blurted out: "He is the blood of my father, you know."

"Who is?" Ebenezer Scrooge asked, but after a moment's thought, he believed he knew.

"Thomas Edward Oldcastle...the man you know as Tom Bray."

"Oh heavens," Scrooge muttered. Could it really be true? He studied the Squire's face looking for any trace of Tom Bray that would suggest a common father but found none. Tom's eyes were large and probing and this man's small and suspicious, and they were built nothing alike. Even when he tried to imagine Mortimer Oldcastle younger and thinner, the contours of both faces in no way matched.

"No one ever knew who his mother was," the Squire went on. "I was thirteen years old when Father brought him into the house, no longer a boy, but not yet a man. Father claimed Tom was a foundling and declared that as the chief landowner in the area, it was his responsibility to take him

156

in. It was not long before I realized that Father, rather than caring for a lost orphan out of duty, doted on Tom, lavishing ever more attention upon him, as though he were the legitimate heir and I the second born."

Thinking of his own strained relationship with his father, Ebenezer Scrooge began to see the landowner in a more sympathetic light.

Now unable to cease his confession, the Squire went on: "Even as a child Tom was different. Once he disappeared into the woods for days at a time, only to be found later living with a family of deer. On another occasion it was with wolves. Then he began to display that peculiar healing power that he has over animals, which made father regard him even more lovingly. 'The boy is a gift,' he would say. In time I was sent off to school while Tom stayed here. Father brought in tutors, but Tom had no ability for traditional learning. He wanted to be near the animals, so he was made stable groom. Thus he has remained ever since."

"And Tom knows nothing of his heritage?" Scrooge asked.

"Nothing. I doubt he could understand what I was saying if I tried to explain it to him. I only learned of the truth conclusively from Father's own lips on his deathbed, though I had long maintained suspicions about their true relationship. It was in my last year of school and I was summoned to my father's bedchamber. There he confessed his duplicity regarding Tom and with his dying breath, he begged me to treat the boy as an equal and love him like a brother. I protested, of course. But then came the most terrible truth of all." The Squire's jowly face quivered and his eyes closed; he put a stubby hand to his head. "Tom Bray may have been the fruit of my father's loins...*but I was not.*"

Squire Oldcastle opened his eyes and looked at Ebenezer Scrooge, a feeble, painful smile managing to escape his lips. "That is the dread secret that has been weighing on my heart, the secret that has aged me ahead of my years and embittered my soul. You see, *I was the foundling*. I was the babe that my father, as lord of the estate, felt duty-bound to rescue. Can you begin to understand my dilemma upon learning the truth? I was about to inherit a vast estate and business, wealth and power, and yet it was not mine to inherit. It was, by the law of blood, the property of a simple stable groom with no greater concept of land ownership than a hawk possesses. A touch of irony, is it not? The only one man alive less naturally suited than I to be the lord of an estate and owner of a factory is the man to whom it truly belongs. I promised Father that I would keep Tom on the property, but I could not jeopardize my new standing by conferring upon the stable groom the status of brother and heir."

"Do you regret that?" Scrooge asked.

"Only in those times when I wish it was *he* who had to deal with the operation of the factory and the production of that nauseating powder that I have come to loathe." Another ironic smile graced the Squire's face. "But really, sir, what would it matter if I did regret it? It is too late now to do anything about it."

In the sprung seat on the back of the hansom, which was speeding through the night skies with the speed of a fired arrow, Tom Bray was completely unaware of his employer's throes of guilt. Instead he was marveling at the sights around him and relishing the cold rush of the wind on his face. The night sky now appeared to be a smoky grey ceiling of clouds that extended in every direction. Tom felt truly lost between two worlds, removed from the only world he had ever known, which was now so far below as to be invisible in the darkness, yet a trespasser in the domain that belonged solely to the birds——and at least one horse. As the white steed drew up to the cloud ceiling, Tom saw that the cottony layer was losing the illusion of solid form, becoming instead a light swirling mist, which soon swallowed the horse, the hansom, and him.

Everything now was grey: grey to the sides of him, grey below him, grey above him, almost as if he had been blindfolded with a moist towel of smoke. A rhythmic sound beat in his ears, which he soon identified as his own heart. Tom sat still and alert as the cab began to slow down.

A light was penetrating the mist, breaking it up and chasing away each swirling tendril, and once again the silhouette of the horse could be seen as the hansom emerged through the clouds.

Inside, Ebenezer Scrooge had also been aware that the vehicle was passing through some kind of dense cloud that had remained invisible against the clear skyscape up until now. He could feel it reach the top of what seemed to be a high hill and then level off, and proceed on smoothly. Looking through the window, he saw that they were now riding upon a flat vaporous expanse. "You must see this," Scrooge said to his traveling companion.

Glancing through the window on his side, Squire Oldcastle was prepared to see the worst imaginings of black hell, but to his surprise he saw instead a lovely cloud landscape complete with diaphanous vales, tors and crags, illuminated by the December half-moon. "Incredible," he uttered, in spite of himself, "this is absolutely... absolutely..."

"Miraculous," Scrooge finished.

"Is this the final irony of man, that upon being transported to the abyss, one must first pass through such wild and exotic beauty?"

Scrooge shook his head. "I wish I could convince you that we are not speeding towards damnation," Scrooge said. "If I am successful we shall *prevent* damnation, and Christmas shall be saved."

"Saved?"

"That is the purpose of this journey, to prevent the world from succumbing to Darkness. My only concern is that we shall not be in time."

The cloud growing inside of Squire Oldcastle's head was as vast and dense as the one supporting them, and he understood not a word his mysterious companion had spoken.

Still peering through the windows, both men saw that they were now traveling down a wide carriage drive seemingly carved out of grey cotton. The drive led to a bank of huge steps centered between towering pillars, which, like the surface of the driveway itself appeared to be constructed not of cloud, but rather of the finest marble. The sudden *clop-clop* of the horse's hooves after so much silence sounded odd and out of place.

As soon as the coach arrived in front of the steps, it stopped. Tom Bray jumped down from the seat and aided Ebenezer Scrooge out first, and then went around for Squire Oldcastle, who looked guiltily at the young man as he stepped out, but said nothing to him. Standing in front of the mysterious edifice of the clouds, Tom asked, "Do we go in?"

"Yes, Tom, we go in," Scrooge said.

"Must we *all* go in?" the Squire inquired, nervously.

"I do not believe we have been united in this miraculous journey through mere chance," Scrooge rejoined. "Unless told otherwise, we should remain together. Follow me." Ebenezer Scrooge started up the stairway, which was effortful for him, given the cold tightness in his chest, which was not abating. *Please let me live long enough to achieve my task*, he silently prayed. At the top the three of them passed through a portal and found themselves inside an enormous rotunda; so large it dwarfed even St. Paul's in London. Constructed of highly polished white marble, or so it appeared, the rotunda was encircled by a ring of stately pillars that stretched further upwards

160

than any of them could see. Squire Oldcastle's mouth dropped open at the magnificence of the rotunda. In between two of the pillars was a massive door, seemingly made of marble, but with no knob or handle. Scrooge moved toward the door with his traveling companions behind him, one of whom——Tom Bray——was willing to follow him anywhere without hesitation, while the other——Squire Oldcastle——took every step as though walking dangerously on the thinly-iced surface of a frozen river. As they approached, the door slowly opened inward, revealing a long passageway, one half of which was brightly illuminated by torches in sconces, and the other half of which was submerged into the densest, darkest shadows Ebenezer Scrooge could ever recall seeing. Miraculously, neither the light nor the darkness encroached into each other's territory, instead remaining a finely-honed separation. As the men strode down the passageway, they themselves reflected the light, or lack thereof, appearing half in light and half in darkness.

"This is incredible," Squire Oldcastle remarked. "I have never seen an environment such as this one."

Yet it has seen you, Scrooge thought; *it has seen all of us.*

From somewhere, the first toll of midnight could be heard. "Dear heavens," Scrooge said, quickening his pace. An opening at the far end of the passageway was now in view, and Scrooge began to run as fast as his legs and wind would allow. He could now hear voices emanating from the chamber beyond the passageway. "My Lord," called a cold and forceful one, "the stroke of midnight is upon us, and the time has expired. We can no longer wait for the imagined champion of this unwanted holiday. If he were coming, he would have arrived by now."

The second toll of midnight struck.

"My Lord," said a softer, mellifluous voice, "we beg your indulgence. There is still time."

161

"Nonsense, My Lord! That is naught but a fairy dream of Helios. I propose we end this now, at this very moment."

The third toll was heard.

"We will wait," said a different voice, one that filled the passageway.

Ebenezer Scrooge was now nearing the entrance to whatever lie beyond, and Tom Bray was but a pace behind him, keeping up step for step. The Squire, however, was far back, huffing and puffing for breath, and cursing each hurried footfall under his voice.

The fourth toll sounded.

At last Scrooge reached the end of the passageway and lurched into the Hall of the Great Tribunal, wheezily declaring, "I have come." Ceasing his run, he became dizzy and was unable to keep from doubling over, both from the exertion of the run and the lightheadedness he was feeling. It was, in fact, all Ebenezer Scrooge could do to keep from collapsing.

"I knew you would not fail us, Ebenezer Scrooge," the mellifluous voice cried.

Tom Bray dashed into the Great Hall and immediately went to his friend to support him, while a moment later, Squire Oldcastle, who was easily as winded as Scrooge, if not more so, staggered into the chamber.

"Look who the champion has brought with him!" the cold, cynical voice said with malicious glee. "It is one of our very own, a most promising, if ignorant, traveler of the Darkness! How accommodating of you, Scrooge."

The fifth toll rang out.

Having managed to catch his breath, Scrooge with Tom's help stood upright and looked around him. Despite everything he had seen over the last two days, the Great Tribunal of the High Justice filled him with awe. Unlike the pillared rotunda and unlike the plain stone-lined passageway through which he had just passed, Ebenezer Scrooge now appeared to be standing out of doors, in the

162

center of a gigantic ring of rough-hewn stones that rose up out of a mist-shrouded floor. The standing stones were as barbaric as the pillars and carved doors had been elegant. Overhead was nothing but a night skyscape of blackness, punctuated by diamond-point stars, and facing him was a freestanding dolmen that resembled an enormous magistrate's bench. Seated behind it was a shadowy figure, so shadowy in fact that Scrooge was unable to determine what manner of being it was. If this was the High Justice, Scrooge was to see no more of him than his rough silhouette.

Standing on each side of the coarse bench were two other figures. One was garbed in a shimmering robe of bright sunlight yellow. The other wore a clinging liquid garment the color of soot. The face of the yellow-garbed figure beamed with warmth and compassion while the other glared at them balefully, a sinister, knowing smile upon its lips. So different were the two demeanors that it was difficult to discern that their features were identical. The face of the Advocate of the Light suddenly beamed brighter, and the Squire spun around and saw that Tom Bray had found his way into the stone circle.

"Now it appears that one of *our* friends has joined us as well," he said. "That makes two against one, I believe."

The sixth toll sounded.

The Advocate of the Light smiled and Tom smiled back. There was a primal power contained within this ring that he was somehow a part of, a power that he could not understand, exactly, yet he accepted. Furthermore, he could tell that it accepted him, and Tom felt comfortable. But when he glanced over at the other figure the smile fell away from his face, and his body tensed under the glowering stare of the Dark Twin. As with the strange tall man in the pub, Tom intuited danger and reacted with a low deliberate exhalation of breath that came out almost as a growl.

The seventh toll of midnight was heard by all.

"Ebenezer Scrooge," the Advocate of the Light began, "you have come so far, but your journey is over. Testify to the Court of humankind's desire for Christmas. We are waiting to hear."

Weakened, aching, tired almost beyond endurance, but standing nevertheless, Ebenezer Scrooge took slow, halting steps towards the dolmen and focused his gaze on the mysterious, shadowy figure at the top. He opened his mouth to speak...but no sound came forth.

The eighth stroke of midnight sounded.

"Please, Ebenezer Scrooge, speak," the Advocate of the Light implored, but Scrooge was no longer capable of delivering a speech; a sudden, sharp, overwhelming pain, like a molten dagger, had just exploded in his heart and robbed him of words. Clutching his chest and moaning, Ebenezer Scrooge sunk to his knees, as the ninth toll of midnight was heard.

"Dear, dear," the Advocate of the Stygios sneered, "it would appear, My Lord, that Helios has suffered something of a setback. It appears that the journey has been too much for my learned Brother's poor, frail witness. In short, My Lord, he is finished."

"What is 'finished'?" Tom Bray demanded of Squire Oldcastle, looking upon the slumping form of Ebenezer Scrooge with helplessness.

"He means, Tom," the Squire replied, "that he is dying."

The tenth toll sounded.

"My Lord," the Advocate of the Dark said, addressing the figure atop the dolmen, "I believe our business here is completed. It is already midnight and——"

"The twelfth stroke has not yet sounded!" the Advocate of the Light interrupted, desperately.

"But it shall, my brother, it shall. If your star witness, who lies before us in a crumpled, dying heap, lives long enough, he shall hear it sound for himself. His last moment

164

of life shall be the ultimate celebration of his complete failure." Facing the Great Judge once more, the Advocate of the Dark said, "My Lord, there is nothing more to be said here. The Age of Darkness has begun!"

The penultimate toll of midnight rang like a death knell.

"My Lord," called Squire Oldcastle, taking a tentative step towards the High Justice, "I should like to speak, if I may."

"This man has not been called as a witness," the Advocate of the Dark said impatiently.

"I call him as a witness, My Lord," interjected the Advocate of the Light, whose face suddenly shone with the light of hope. "I further request that the final knell not be struck until his testimony has been heard."

"Does Stygios object?" intoned the High Justice.

After a moment's thought, the Advocate of the Dark said: "Object, My Lord? Not at all. This traveler is well known to us, as are his views of the foolish holiday whose future we are here to decide. By all means, let him speak." Turning to Squire Oldcastle, who shrank under his withering gaze, the Advocate said, "Tell us, my friend in Darkness, just how much *Christmas* has meant to you." The Advocate of the Dark spoke the word *Christmas* as though it caused him pain.

"Speak now," the High Justice said.

Facing the "bench," the Squire began. "Your honor...your grace...your lordship...your *Yourness*, you see before you a man who has denied Christmas, lo, these many years. I have never had the time for it, and there are many, many more like me."

The face of the Advocate of the Dark broke into a broad smile that was somehow more terrible than his scowl. "My Lord, here is the testimony for which we have been waiting. You have heard the judgment of Humankind."

"I have not yet finished," the Squire interjected.

From the earthen floor of the chamber Ebenezer Scrooge, gasping and in agony but still alive, struggled to raise his eyes until they met those of the Advocate of the Light, who looked back hopefully.

Squire Oldcastle continued: "As I was saying, I have long felt that Christmas was a day honored only by fools." At that moment, Mortimer Oldcastle, respected landowner and country Squire, did something he had never done before in his life: he giggled. It was a sound that bubbled up from deep inside him and erupted from his lips like lava from a volcano, as his round body shook like a Christmas pudding. "Your Honor," he shouted, "if Christmas is for fools only, then may I be the greatest fool in the history of the world! *Hee hee hee hee*!"

The smug face of the Advocate of the Dark changed instantly into a mask of cold fury. "My Lord, this man is mad! He is not qualified to testify."

"He *is* qualified, My Lord, eminently so!" said the Advocate of the Light. "I pray you let him continue."

"Continue," the sepulchral voice of the Tribunal ordered.

"Yes, yes, of course," the Squire said, unable to suppress another giggle. "If you take away Christmas, Your Honor, you take away hope. If you take away hope and you render the human animal nothing more than a drudge and a beast!"

"What *is* the human animal if not a drudge and a beast!" argued the Advocate of the Dark.

"What is it, you ask?" the Squire answered. "Why, the human animal is knowledge and melancholy and hope and ignorance and sloth and brilliance and each one the controllers of his or her own destiny. That is the human animal, Your Honor!"

"*You have changed*!" the Advocate of the Dark spat.

"Yes, I have changed. Or rather, I have come to my senses. For too long my life has been governed by fear and

I have lived without joy. This night I dared to believe that there might actually be a chance of redemption for me, and lo, I have found it! Yes, you great black goat, I have changed! For what does it mean to be human if one cannot change? Bad to good, good to bad, it almost matters not; what matters is that we are masters of our own lives and destinies, and no one can take that away from us. If you eradicate Christmas, Your Honor, you erase any hope that life can be better. You ask if we poor human creatures want Christmas, need Christmas, require Christmas? Yes! Your Honor, yes! Christmas, and every holiday of hope and joy like it, celebrated by any people across the Earth!"

Squire Oldcastle then fell silent. The Advocates of Light and Dark neither moved nor spoke, but each stood regarding him in his own way. As for Ebenezer Scrooge, the fire in his chest had been replaced by numbness, and the circle of stones appeared to spin around him. His head felt light, as though it might separate itself from his shoulders and float away. But even so, he forced himself to rise, aided by Tom Bray, who had remained by his side since entering the rustic chamber.

"My Lord," Scrooge panted, "I am but a man, one man, no more, no less. Whether I shall even see the morrow or not, I cannot say. But I swear upon…upon the judgment of this court…that when my time comes to go into the dust of the earth, I will go singing of Christmas. I will——" Another sudden spasm racked his body and Scrooge fell limp in the arms of Tom Bray, who gently lowered him to the floor. He tried laying his hands on the barely-breathing figure, but it did no good. His friend was a man, not an animal. Tears began to form in Tom's eyes.

All was silence. Time stood in place. The voice of the Great Judge commanded, "Come forward," and the two Advocates approached the dolmen. "After hearing all the evidence, I have reached a decision. Based upon the testimony I have heard from the witnesses, it is my judgment that Christmas *shall remain.*"

The final toll of midnight struck. It was December the twenty-fifth; Christmas Day.

There was utter silence in the Courtroom. No one cheered, no one danced in victory, nor howled in defeat, no one offered congratulations or recriminations. All simply let the victory and all it meant slowly seep into them.

The silence was finally broken by the Advocate of the Dark. "So, my brother," he sneered, addressing his opponent, "you appear to have won the battle, but not the war. My Master will never allow that to happen."

"Nor will mine," the Advocate of the Light replied, "as your master well understands."

"Lord Tenebra will not be pleased with the results of this adventure. Your Lord of Light had better prepare himself for the battles that are to come."

The Light Twin smiled. "He is always prepared, as are his armies."

Now Tom Bray spoke up. "What of Ebenezer?" he demanded, wiping his eyes as he rose to confront the Advocates. "What about him?"

The Advocate of the Light smiled warmly, but the warmth bore Tom no comfort. "He will go back to the place from whence he started, as will you," he said. Then turning to Squire Oldcastle, he added: "And you as well, my newly recruited foot soldier. Everything will go back the way it began," the Advocate said, adding: "*Almost.*"

"What does he mean?" Squire Oldcastle demanded, but no one answered. No one had the chance to answer.

In the next instant, all was gone. There was nothingness; absolute white nothingness.

SIXTEEN

Dawn on Christmas morning broke very cold and damp.

Traces of a thin frost blanket remained on the ground with patches of earth and stone showing through its worn places. It was the sort of English morning to be sleeping in the warm comfort of one's own bed, yet when Mortimer Oldcastle awoke, he did so huddled and shivering on the seat of his family coach, which remained disabled on the country road that serviced the village. Cold and disoriented, he examined his surroundings, desperately trying to force his mind to make some sense of things. Getting out, he spied the broken wheel and a memory began to emerge, as though from a dream, of his racing into the woods in pursuit of the coach, which had been...

"Stolen," he muttered. "Great Gods, have I spent the entire night out here? If so, where are the others, that man..."

It was then that Squire Oldcastle remembered everything.

"Did it really happen?" he asked himself. "*Could* it have really happened?"

With a rare shout of delight simply at being alive on a bright, bracing morning, Mortimer Oldcastle began to run down the road toward the manor house, hoping to find answers to his questions.

Not far away, in the stable house of Oldcastle Manor, Tom Bray lay curled and sleeping on the straw-strewn floor of one of the horse stalls. A gentle nudge from the nose of a black horse roused Tom and, as was his custom, he awoke instantly and surveyed his surroundings. His body was sore and stiff and after a moment he recalled the dream in which he had soared through the night sky and had listened to the chimes at midnight in a strange but somehow powerful circle of standing stones. Had it really been a dream? He thought harder, trying to pull the previous night into sharper focus. The last memory Tom had was of the smiling face of a strange man who seemed to like him. How had he ended up in the stable? Taking in a series of deep breaths to help clarify his mind, he searched for an answer, at first getting nothing but confusion in return. Then the solution, the only possible solution, presented itself to him and he understood completely.

After stroking the horse's face and withers affectionately, Tom ran out of the stable and started for his hut, only to hear the sound of running footsteps coming toward him. Tom Bray was not a man who startled easily, but the sight of Squire Oldcastle waving at him as he trotted down the wooded road, a broad smile on his broader face, gave him pause.

"Tom! Tom Bray!" the Squire called. "Wait for me!"

Huffing and puffing, the rotund man finally made his way to Tom as the bell from the old village church began to toll. "Did it really happen, Tom?" the Squire asked urgently. "Tell me it really happened!"

Tom Bray nodded, a slight smile breaking on his lips.

"It happened! It really happened! And then we fell from the sky, unharmed! *Ha ha ha*! *Hee hee hee*!" He continued to laugh until tears ran from his eyes, and then embraced the true scion of Oldcastle, who accepted the gesture of affection stiffly, being unused to such attention. "Yes, Tom, we spent midnight in the heavens, you and I, only to sail down like great fat pigeons jarred from a roost and land back home unharmed. Impossible, you say?" Tom Bray had said nothing of the kind, but the Squire babbled on: "Yes, it is impossible! *All* miracles are impossible! At least that's what they try to tell us, isn't it, my boy? Oh, they do try to tell us that the only true things on earth are toil and misery and sickness, and that all else is merely an illusion, an impossibility, but we won't listen, will we Tom? Will we, Mr. Bray? *Hee hee hee!* No, we won't listen to them!"

Finding it impossible not to grin, Tom nodded in agreement.

"Do you know why this impossibility, this miracle occurred?" the Squire asked jovially. "Because that is the only way we could have made it back in time for Christmas! And it is Christmas, is it not? Tell me we have not missed Christmas!"

In answer to his question the chimes in the church tower put forth a sweet golden carol, the music of the bells lifting the clouds and brightening the morning gloom considerably.

"We have not missed it!" the Squire cried, spinning in a circle until he became too dizzy to continue. "*Ha ha*! We have not missed Christmas! *Ha ha*! *Hee hee hee*!" The Squire leapt into the air, then somersaulted, then jumped and clicked his heels together, or at least as close together as his heels would come.

The Squire had changed, no doubt about that. It wasn't simply that he was now filled with joy, though that was surprising enough; there was a physical difference in the little man that was plain as paint to anyone who cared to see it. The coating of chill surrounding him had cracked and peeled away, and his eyes cast off a light instead of sucking it in from others and turning it to dusk. Anyone would have encountered him the day before, and then again today, would be justified in their puzzlement over how a man could *youthen* overnight.

But that was not the only change that had come of the new day: marveling at the actions of his employer the

171

Squire, Tom Bray himself felt different. He had to admit, if to no one but himself, that he was actually enjoying watching the laughing, cartwheeling man. He almost wanted to join in. For the first time in his life Tom Bray desired to know more about and be around the strange race of creatures that he had accidentally been born into. He had *understood* things for so long, but now he wanted to *know*.

Behind them, unchanged by the day and unmoved by it all, stood Oldcastle Hall, smoke curling up from its chimneys and disappearing into the granite sky.

Nearly exhausted from his acrobatics, Mortimer Oldcastle approached Tom and embraced him like a brother. "We have many things to talk about, Tom. Heaven be praised that we have the time to do so. And heaven be praised for that strange man——the man who wasn't there! Wasn't there, indeed! *Ha ha!*"

Tom suddenly stiffened. *That strange man. Ebenezer. His friend. Where was he?* His face a mask of concern, Tom dashed away and began to examine the manor grounds like a hound.

"What are you looking for?" the Squire asked.

"Ebenezer."

"He must be around here somewhere, I shouldn't wonder. After all, how far could he have fallen?" Unable to suppress another giggle——the humor of which was not shared by the stable groom, whose face darkened even further——the Squire then joined in the search, looking behind stones and peering around the other sides of trees and bushes.

Another pair of eyes was watching this curious dawn hide-and-seek game with growing trepidation. In the early hours of morning Osmund had been alerted by Lady Oldcastle that the master had not returned home. Since then the servant had been engaged in a hunt of his own and had nearly given up when he noticed two figures bursting forth from the stable. Upon closer inspection they revealed

172

themselves as his master and the groom, which calmed Osmund's alarm and, he hoped, his mistress's fears. But on second glance their activities, particularly the master's, concerned him greatly.

Osmund's thin form was concealed behind a tree some little distance away, a vantage point from which he had watched the silent display of dancing and leaping and embracing and laughing with growing dismay. At long last it had happened: His master's mind, which he had heard spoken of so frequently as being as fragile as an egg when taxed by inferiors, had finally cracked. In short, he was mad as a coot! And as the household chief of staff, it fell to him to find a way to explain to her ladyship that the master was, as they say in the finer establishments of the London, *barking*. But how should he broach the subject? The very thought of facing her ladyship while Squire Oldcastle was somersaulting across the yard and laughing like a lunatic made his stomach hurt.

Thinking it best to approach the tragedy, Osmund stepped out from behind his tree and loped towards the apparent madman with as much dignity as he could muster. He tentatively called to him but the Squire took no notice as he moved towards a clump of ash trees, inspecting every foot of ground along the way. "M'lord?" the servant called again.

"Hmmm? What is it?" said the Squire, turning to face him. In the past he had usually addressed the tall servant's midriff when speaking to him, since he did not believe in looking up to a menial, but now he gazed straight into Osmund's eyes, and his doughy face brightened. "Ah, Osmund, my good man. Merry Christmas to you!" he exclaimed, clasping the hand of the servant and pumping it exuberantly.

"Pardon me for asking, sir, but are you well?"

"Yes, yes, of course!" Squire Oldcastle replied brightly, "why would I not be? It is, after all, Christmas!"

173

Closing one eye and rattling his head so sharply that it nearly fell off, the servant said: "I beg pardon, m'lord?"

Laughing heartily, the Squire wrapped his arms around Osmund——who may have been the only person in creation thin enough for the Squire to put his arms around——and bade him Merry Christmas! and Merry Christmas! again. Unused to this kind of charity from his employer, or *any* kind of charity from him for that matter, the servant did not quite know what to say. Standing tall and straight as a maypole, around which the Squire cavorted, he finally uttered: "Forgive me for saying so, m'lord, but I fear this must be said: you do not seem quite yourself this morning."

All joviality suddenly left the round man's face. He glared into the manservant's eyes with an expression of utmost seriousness. "Do I not?" he asked gravely.

"No sir, I fear you do not."

"I see. There is only one thing I can say to that." The face of the Squire then burst into a holiday wreath of joy and he shouted: "*Good*!" He pumped Osmund's hand again, chiding, "Why do you look so concerned, dear boy? It is Christmas Day!"

Raving, stark, staring mad, the servant thought; *but on the other hand, a decided improvement*. As long as the master did not become violent, it might just be an insanity he could live with. However, it *was* a bad morning to be out. "Sir, I do feel you should come inside. It is quite crisp out here this morning, and I fear you shall catch your death——"

"No, my good man, no!" the Squire interrupted. "You do not understand. I have only just caught my *life*! In fact, I am burning up with the fever of it! All those years that I let life slide past me, discarding most days unused, never realizing how much more there was…I realize it now. I have changed, Osmund; do not ask me how, for I am not sure I can tell you. It was a miracle, I shouldn't wonder!

174

But having so changed, I shall spend the rest of my days working to help others change as well!"

Osmund regarded him as a candidate for Bedlam.

"I see you looking skeptical, sir," the Squire said, correctly assessing his servant's thoughts. "But things will change, that I vow! *Hee hee hee*! It will begin with Matilda and myself. She is at heart a good woman, Osmund. The years she has spent with me have soured her personality, but it will be different now. By next Christmas she will be a new woman, I shouldn't wonder. Come, my emaciated friend, let us go inside." The Squire placed a hand on his servant's shoulder. "It is fearful cold. Tom! Tom, come along inside. We will fortify ourselves in the kitchen and then resume the search for your friend."

"He is not here," Tom said, grimly. He could not *sense* Ebenezer Scrooge.

"Then that makes the situation even simpler," Squire Oldcastle said. "Come along, my boy, come inside."

Osmund rattled his head once more, trying to make sense of the fact that his master had actually invited Tom Bray into the house. Except for occasional appearances in the servant's kitchen, Osmund did not believe Tom had seen the interior of the manor since childhood.

Having finally persuaded Tom to join them, the Squire virtually bounced up the carriage drive like a ball, prattling away about Christmas, until the groom Tom stopped suddenly and listened intently to the wind.

"What is it?" asked Osmund

"Horse is coming."

"I do not hear anything." But within seconds the servant was able to make out the distant shape galloping around the wooded curve, heading towards them. "I see it," he exclaimed, "it is a coach, somewhat smaller than yours, m'lord."

"Yes, my coach," the Squire said. "I must send the village wheelwright out to fix it, but not today. Oh ho, not on Christmas day! Tomorrow will be soon enough."

"As you say, m'lord," Osmund replied, still reeling from the developments of the morning. Looking toward the sound of the oncoming vehicle, he said, "it appears to be a city cabriolet, of all things."

"Can you see who is driving?"

"Traveler," said Tom Bray.

"That would stand to reason," Osmund rejoined.

"No. *Traveler*. Man from last night."

The carriage was now near enough for all of them to see that it was indeed a hansom; looking very much like the one Tom had driven to the court in the sky, driven by the man in the Ulster coat and short top hat. Reining the snowy white horse to a halt, the drive said, "I am so glad I found you, Mr. Bray. We must leave for London."

"Does it concern that man Ebenezer?" the Squire asked.

"Yes sir, it does," the driver replied.

"Is he all right?"

"All I know, sir, is that I need to get Tom Bray to the city, and quickly." He gestured to Tom.

"I shall come, too."

"No, sir, you're to stay here. There are things for you to do here."

"Yes, my good man, I suppose there are at that," the Squire said. Then stepping to Tom Bray, he placed a hand on the young man's shoulder. "You must go with him, Tom. Do whatever you are told to do and then come back here as soon as you are finished. There is much we have to talk about."

Tom nodded and rushed to the cab, where he started to climb up into the sprung seat. "No, sir, you must get inside," the driver told him.

Tentatively, as if he was doing something bad for which he would be caught and punished, Tom Bray stepped down and then climbed inside the cab and for the first time in his life, sat like a gentleman. The seat did not fit as badly as he had expected.

Without another word, the driver pulled the cab around, whipped the horse into action, and headed off toward the city. "Oh, and another thing!" the Squire called after him, "*Merry Christmas*!" Dabbing at his frosted strawberry nose, he told Osmund: "I do indeed know what I must do to help that strange man, that wonderful man whose acquaintance I made last evening. Had I been doing so for these past many years, I daresay I could have saved the fellow a great deal of trouble. But it is never too late, eh, my friend?" He slapped a benevolent hand on the back of the servant, who smiled back with new appreciation for his master, if no less bafflement regarding his actions. Perhaps someday, Osmund mused, it would be his privilege to understand.

"What is the time?" the Squire asked.

Ceremoniously taking out his watch and popping open the lid, the servant announced that it was some five minutes before seven.

"Seven! Seven o'clock, is it? Well, then, my good man, we must hurry if we are going to accomplish anything! The men are not yet at the factory, is that right?"

"Not for another hour."

"Good. Then send Mervyn down there to close it."

Osmund shook his head, not certain he had heard correctly. "Close the factory?"

"Yes, close it. It is Christmas, man, Christmas! Send the workers home——no, wait! Tell them to come here to the manor. We shall prepare a feast, the finest holiday feast this village has ever seen! Tell them to bring their families! How many would that be? Oh, what does it matter, it is Christmas! That table in the main hall must be able to seat a hundred at a time, I shouldn't wonder. *Ha!*"

"May I ask what this feast will consist of?"

"Goose and dressing and pudding and roast pig and muffins and mince pie and...and...and..."

"And broiled oysters on toast," the servant said, licking his thin lips.

"Yes, of course, and more! Send Mrs. Kenley to town and tell her to buy whatever she needs to make it the grandest feast in the history of the county! Tell her to rouse the shop owners if they have closed! Come along, man, we must go to work!"

And the two raced all the way up to the front door of the hall. Surprisingly, the Squire won.

As the banquet of the century was being prepared in the rapidly warming halls of Oldcastle Manor, Tom Bray sat in the speeding hansom on his way to London. The currents of his mind flowed in a single direction that pointed the way to Ebenezer, his friend, who still needed him.

Tom thought of nothing else as he sped through the countryside, whose verdant hills and woods were dusted with snow. Whenever the vehicle rolled past a field, be it filled with cows, sheep or horses, the beasts would look up and follow the path of the cab with their eyes, as though aware of the occupant inside. Tom did not notice; his thoughts remained centered on his friend, Ebenezer Scrooge, and they were deflected away only as the open expanse around him began to meld into civilization; simple villages at first, not unlike his own, but then the beginnings of a great city, with rows of houses giving way to a maze of buildings.

By the time he had passed into the confines of the great city, Tom Bray rode with his head thrust outside of the cab, gaping in amazement at the sheer volume of life in London. Everywhere around him were the trappings and the spirit of Christmas: holly wreaths and boughs were hung on front doors; further down the block a boy struggled to navigate the street with a tree nearly twice his size, assisted by a small dog that leapt and yipped happily at this feet; further on, a woman carried a stack of brightly-ribboned packages. Everywhere men tipped hats and shook hands. He had never seen a day like this.

Not long after the vehicle had sped past the enormous domed presence of St. Paul's Cathedral, it came to a halt in front of a plain looking house, outside of which a gathering of silent, solemn people had collected. The door of the cab opened up and the driver said: "We are here, sir." Tom stepped out and looked at the crowd of people, not knowing what to do, but sensing that the men, women and children standing by the street on this cold morning were there for his friend.

"You are Tom," a voice said, and Tom looked over to see a very young man limping toward him. Slender and frail, like a lame deer, the boy's face looked a great deal like that of the man named Peter who had called his friend "uncle." "My name is Timothy," the boy said, reaching out to take Tom's arm. "We have been waiting for you?"

"For me?" Tom asked.

The boy nodded. "The rest are here. Come." He led Tom through the crowd of people gathered by the front door of Ebenezer Scrooge's house and on into the house, up the wide staircase, and into a bedchamber where another group of people had gathered. Tom knew none of them. The only person he recognized was the still, waxen figure lying in the canopy bed: it was his friend, now on death's door.

"Ebenezer!" Tom called out.

"Save your breath, he cannot hear you," said a large, stout man with a black beard, grooming that identified him as a physician. "He is beyond hearing now."

"Why?" Tom demanded, unable to articulate his real question, which is why the man in whose company he had traveled to the mysterious courtroom located high above the earth, perhaps even high above the comprehension of mortal man, had found himself in dire straits back in the cold, hard world, miles and miles away from the village in which he had last been seen.

An older man stepped forward, one whose face possessed the same qualities of the boy named Timothy and the man named Peter. "Mr. Scrooge was discovered early this morning lying beneath an open window, nearly frozen," Bob Cratchit told Tom. "It appears that his heart has given out. Are you a friend of his?"

"Yes," Tom replied, "his friend." He looked to Timothy Cratchit with an expression of confusion: if he was, as the boy said, expected, why did this man appear not to know who he was?

"This man is known to me, father," Tim said. "His name is Tom."

"Very well, any friend of yours, Tim, is welcome here," Bob said, somberly introducing himself to Tom and then pointing out his other son Daniel and his daughter Belinda, who was daubing her eyes with a handkerchief as she leaned against her husband. "And that," Bob Cratchit added, pointing to a man seated on a stool in the corner, "is Mr. Scrooge's nephew, Fred."

Fred Billings sat in the crowded bedroom still and inconsolable. "If only I had returned last night, there might have been time to save him," he muttered. "If only I had not remained at the hospital with that unfortunate girl."

Moving to him, Bob Cratchit put a hand on his shoulder and said, "Fred, you must stop this. It is not your fault. He has been ill of late. It is time."

Now another man burst into the room, and this one Tom recognized immediately: Peter Cratchit. "Father, how is he?"

"Peter," Bob said, rushing to his son to take his hand, "I was worried you would not arrive in time. Where have you been?"

"I was out of the city. I came as soon as I heard. I was——" Peter ceased speaking when he spotted Tom Bray standing in the bedchamber. "I was with him, actually," he said, in wonderment. "How did Tom get here?"

"News of this sort travels fast, brother," Tim Cratchit said. "Uncle Ebenezer is, alas, at death's door."

Tom Bray gasped.

"Is there nothing that can be done?" Peter Cratchit asked.

"Nothing at all," black-bearded Dr. Emerson Leach said, packing up his medical instruments.

"Dr. Leach has examined Ebenezer fully," Bob Cratchit explained. "I am afraid it is hopeless."

"He is in the hands of one more powerful than I," Dr. Leach pronounced. "I am very sorry." Picking up his worn leather bag, he exited the room.

Tim Cratchit went over to Tom and said, "He cannot help Ebenezer, Tom, but you can."

The groom looked back at the small, frail young man with a puzzled expression. "Me? Help him?"

Tim Cratchit nodded.

Then a sudden exchange of words from the hall shattered the quiet of the bedroom. "Here now, you cannot take that creature in there, I forbid it!" the physician's voice was shouting. That was followed by a youthful, defiant voice crying, "It ain't no creature, it's 'is blinkin' cat!"

"I don't care what it is," Dr. Leach thundered, "you cannot take it in there! Stop, you little street urchin!"

The small figure of Joby Partle suddenly darted to the room carrying with him a calico cat. "I found her cryin' outside my mum's door," he said. "She wants to be 'ere with 'er master!" He ran to Bob Cratchit, tears rolling down his smudged face. "Honest, mister, 'e'd've wanted 'er 'ere."

The doctor charged in after him. "I will not have that poor man's last moments on earth spoiled by the presence of a dirty street animal!" he bellowed, grabbing the boy's arm and shaking the cat loose. Fanny sprang away, running

181

in-and-around all the people in the room before springing up onto the bed, landing on the chest of Ebenezer Scrooge. "Now look what you've done, you little imp!"

Joby reached for the cat, but it leapt off Ebenezer Scrooge and dashed under the bed. Bending down, Joby reached for her, and was shocked by the cat's panicked hiss.

"Yeow!" Joby shouted, jumping back from the bed. "She clawed me!" He looked at his scratched and bleeding hand, and tears formed in his eyes. "She ain't never done that before," he said in a hurt voice.

"Serves you perfectly right, you——"

"The boy has done nothing wrong," Tim said with startling authority, and the physician's mouth snapped shut.

Kneeling down to comfort the sobbing Joby, Tim said, much more gently, "She is frightened, that is why she scratched you. Animals are different from us. They feel things and sense things that we do not." Then he looked up at the large man and said, "Isn't that right, Tom?"

Tom Bray nodded in agreement.

"In her own way," Tim went on, "she knows Uncle Ebenezer is very ill, and that upsets her. I think she is also very sorry that she hurt you, because she loves you, too. Isn't that right, Tom?"

Tom looked at the bed as if he could see through it and view the cat underneath, and then looked back and again nodded.

Rising with some effort, given his weak legs, Tim Cratchit gently took Joby by the arm and walked him to Dr. Leach. "See to the scratch," he instructed, and the physician began to respond, but thought better, and then quietly went to his bag for salve.

A woman now appeared in the doorway of the bedroom. "Joby, what are you doing in here?" she demanded.

182

"It is all right, Mrs. Partle," Bob Cratchit said to Joby's mother. "He is not disturbing anything."

"I got scratched is all," the boy said.

The woman turned to leave again, but was stopped by Tim. "Stay here with us," he said. "We will need you." Then he turned to Joby, whose hand was being bandaged by the doctor. "I think that if Uncle Scrooge knew Fanny was in the room with him, it would make him feel better. His circle would be complete." Glancing up at Tom Bray, he reiterated: "His *circle*. Isn't that so, Tom?"

Tom thought for a moment, then an expression of understanding crossed his face, and without a word he stepped to the bed, knelt down and reached underneath it.

"Careful, young man," Bob Cratchit said, "or you will be scratched, too."

"No," Tom replied, as he gingerly pulled out the docile calico and cradled her in his large arms. The cat's eyes were moist, as if she too were crying. Tom gently stroked her head as he sat on the edge of the sickbed.

"Here now, what do you think you are doing?" Dr. Leach demanded, swabbing salve on Joby's hurt hand. "Get that creature away from him!"

"He knows what he's doing," Tim Cratchit declared, and his father was helpless to do anything but look to his other children and shrug in wonderment.

Tom Bray placed the calico in Scrooge's lap and carefully draped one of the old man's hands around her. The cat immediately started purring. Then Tom placed one hand under Scrooge's neck, supporting his head. The other he held out and said, "Take it." At first no one made a move, but then Peter Cratchit stepped to him and grasped Tom's hand in his own. A second later his father joined him, puzzled but helpless to resist, and held his hand out for his son Daniel, who in turn extended his hand to Fred Billings.

"What is this?" Dr. Leach demanded, as Tim Cratchit placed himself on the other side of the bed and gently placed a hand on Ebenezer Scrooge's forehead, then held out his other hand, which was quickly taken by Joby Partle, then by his mother. One by one, the others in the room ringed around the bed, joining hands. Only at the foot of the bed was there a break and only Dr. Leach remained out of the circle.

"Exactly what good do you expect this will do?" the physician asked brusquely.

"What harm will it do?" Tim Cratchit countered.

"The circle must close," Tom Bray said.

"This is absurd," Dr. Leach sneered, but he slowly approached the bed and took a hand in each of his to close the circle.

For several minutes no one spoke, no one moved and nothing happened. Then the thin hand of Ebenezer Scrooge twitched and tentatively began to stroke the fur of the cat, which began to purr more loudly and with more delight than any cat before it or any cat since.

"Great God," Dr. Leach whispered, "he is opening his eyes!"

Indeed, the tired eyes of Ebenezer Scrooge were opened, and he regarded the circle with some bewilderment. "My friends," he uttered weakly, "what is the occasion?"

"Christmas, dear Uncle Ebenezer," Fred Billings said. "The grandest, most glorious, most blessed Christmas ever!"

Seeing his feline pet Scrooge said, "Do you hear that, Fanny? It is Christmas. I haven't missed it." Then raising his eyes upwards, he said, "I haven't missed it, my darling Fan,"

At once the circle of men and women broke into a dozen pieces, each one shouting and laughing and leaping and weeping and singing…not to mention meowing.

184

"Scrooge!" the physician said, rushing from the foot of the bed to his side, "I cannot believe it! How are you feeling?"

In a hoarse rasp, Ebenezer Scrooge replied, "I feel like a veal cutlet that has been pounded for breading. I feel like every breath I take is not comprised of air, but rather of broken glass. I feel like the very hairs on my head are causing me distress…and I have never felt more wonderful in my life."

Amidst the joyful weeping in the bedroom, Bob Cratchit dashed to the window, threw it open and shouted to the crowd gathered below on the street: "He will live! Ebenezer Scrooge will live!" The cheering from the people, young and old, rich and poor alike, mingled with the sound of merriment coming from the bedroom.

It was a Christmas day that many would remember for a long, long time.